VENGEANCE IS ALSO MINE

'A good copper, but too inclined to become emotionally involved,' was his colleagues' opinion of Detective Inspector Sander. This trait was stronger than ever after he had met the tragic family of a young man gunned down in a bank raid, particularly as he was sure of the identity of the gunmen – but could not prove it. Paradoxically, when someone began to exact vengeance on the gunmen in his own peculiar ways, it was then Sander's duty to protect the killers he knew from the killer who hunted them...

VENGEANCE IS ALSO MINE

VENGEANCE IS ALSO MINE

by

Will Palmer

Dales Large Print Books
Long Preston, North Yorkshire,
BD23 4ND, England.

British Library Cataloguing in Publication Data.

Palmer, Will
    Vengeance is also mine.

    A catalogue record of this book is
    available from the British Library

    ISBN 1-84262-477-6 pbk

First published in Great Britain in 1980 by Robert Hale Ltd.

Copyright © Will Palmer 1980

The moral right of the author has been asserted

Published in Large Print 2006 by arrangement with
Robert Hale Limited

Dales Large Print is an imprint of Library Magna Books Ltd.

Printed and bound in Great Britain by
T.J. (International) Ltd., Cornwall, PL28 8RW

PART ONE

Cause

1

'Sod this job,' Inspector Jack Sander said with real feeling.

From the other side of the room, Detective Sergeant Gary Blackman glanced across at him with a trained, impassive face. The Old Man was at it again. He should be used to it by now, this odd softness the Inspector had when it came to dealing with the victims of crimes of violence, but he was not. A sign of weakness, he thought. All his training had stressed, no personal involvement on either side. It clouded the issue and the judgement.

Wisely, he kept his opinions to himself. Sander's well-known weakness for one section of the population was seldom applied to any other – least of all newly-promoted Detective Sergeants. Instead, he switched his glance to cover the cheaply-furnished room and offered a non-committal 'They haven't got very much, have they?'

'They've got even less now,' Sander grunted sourly and belligerently, inviting further provocation.

Blackman sighed internally, fixed his gaze on a very uninteresting, mass-produced sideboard as though it were a work of art and took the subordinate's easy way out – silence. It would pass.

Sander kept his hot, brown eyes on him for a few more moments. He was aware that he was being unreasonable, Gary was a good lad, but there was little that he could do about it when this feeling came over him. It had not changed in twenty years. It was the same now as the first time he had shuffled into a not-too-clean kitchen, twisted his helmet in awkward hands and told a wide-eyed woman that her small son had been killed in a cycling accident. Her hurt, disbelieving, why-me look had planted itself in his mind and stayed ever since and he had seen it repeated in the faces of all the victims he had spoken to over the intervening years. Some got used to it. He never had. Idly he wondered about the poor bugger who had delivered today's news. How had he told the Maxwell family that their son had intervened in an armed, bank robbery and had half his chest blown away by the short range blast of a sawn-off, twelve-bore shotgun? Not quite like that, he hoped.

He pushed the thought away, took his eyes from Blackman and let them wander round the room. He was right, they had not got much. A three piece suite that cost a lot less than a hundred pounds about ten years ago, a carpet which matched neither the curtains or the wallpaper and a veneered-oak sideboard that years of patient polishing had failed to improve. Not much at all. And, Christ it was cold in here.

He bent, rubbed his hands briskly in front of the imitation-log fire then straightened and looked at the shelf above it. Nothing much there either. A pair of vases which could only have been an unwanted wedding present, a clock which was ten minutes slow and a collection of framed photographs. There were four in all. A big-boned, dark-haired woman in her forties smiling self-consciously into the camera while she draped her arm around a girl who was a younger replica of herself. A girl with too much character in her face to be called pretty and too much liveliness to be called plain. Beside that, was a picture of a young man. Mid-twenties, big-boned and dark like the woman, he wore the uniform of the Parachute Regiment and looked out from the photograph with an attempt at the dignity that the uniform and the occasion demanded without quite succeeding. The two portraits in matching positions on the other side of the shelf were also of men. One was another big-built, dark, young man with a cheery grin so similar to the others that there was no need for Sander's mind to query his identity. This would be him – had been him – Mark Maxwell, alive and perhaps grinning in the same fashion this morning, now something on a slide-out tray in a mortuary and whatever expression was on his face, fixed there forever. He sighed and switched to the last picture. It was much older than all the others. Little more than a blown-up snapshot faded by years of light. It showed another young man and another uniform, open-necked regulation shirt with a field service cap tucked neatly but ostentatiously under a shoulder epaulette so that the regimental badge showed clearly. It was obviously an amateur effort but it had captured the features well and Sander studied them closely. He had great belief in what could be seen in a man's face and there was a lot to see in this one. Fairer than all the others, it was thin and fine-boned. A face which was sensitive but at the same time hinted of an inner toughness of spirit that might bend and tremble but never break. The sort of face that Sander had grown to be wary of over the past twenty years. It would be a bit shy and self-effacing and probably never cause trouble but there was a hint of the fanatic who would be diverted by nothing once he had decided that his course of action was in the right. A face to pick out in a meeting or a protest or a demonstration and keep a careful eye on.

The opening of a door and the entrance of a woman pulled his eyes and mind from their study of the picture. She was a small, dumpy woman, permed, brown hair shading to a smattering of grey. She wore a wrap around, floral apron and a tentative, out-of-her-depth, half smile.

'Mrs Maxwell will be down in a minute,' she said a little hesitantly. 'Er, just freshening herself up – you know.'

'Yes. Of course. Thank you Mrs – er.' For the life of him, Sander could not remember the name the woman had tossed at them when she allowed them in the house.

'Checksfield,' she supplied.

11

'Ah yes. Very good of you to come in and lend a hand like this Mrs Checksfield.'

'Well your man came next door and asked me after he had brought them the news,' she said simply and then, realising how the statement had sounded, hurried on. 'Of course, I'd have come in anyway. What are neighbours for if you can't turn to them in times like this?'

'Quite, but not everyone thinks like that, I'm afraid, Mrs Checksfield.'

'Well I do. I've always said to our Bob...'

'Yes, yes,' Sander cut in. He had little interest in what Mrs Checksfield always told her Bob. 'You say Mrs Maxwell will be down. Mr Maxwell isn't at home then?'

'Oh yes. But I don't think he'll come down – poor dear. He was already under the doctor before the – this news. This has just about knocked him out.'

'Suffers from ill health does he?'

'Oh not strong – not strong at all,' Mrs Checksfield confided. 'Been like it for years. Every winter he goes down and every winter it seems worse. Something to do with something he got during the war, the doctor says. He was a prisoner you know with the Japanese and that lot out east. Wounded and everything, Bob says. He never says much about it

12

but he does say a bit to Bob from time to time, him having been in the army an all you know. Like I said, this has just about floored him.'

Sander's eyes found their way back to the photograph for a quick moment. So he had cracked. Ah well, he had been wrong before and would be again, he supposed.

'It's a bad blow,' he said as though excusing his own judgement.

'Terrible thing,' Mrs Checksfield agreed. 'Terrible thing. That poor boy – and such a nice boy too, always so polite and friendly. And those poor people upstairs. Oh it makes you wonder what the world's coming to sometimes.'

Sander had stopped wondering many years ago but he nodded and there was a little, awkward silence. A silence Mrs Checksfield could not endure for long.

'Isn't it cold in here?' She bustled across the room and turned up the gas fire then rubbed her hands together. 'That's better. Perhaps a cup of tea Inspector?'

'Er, no thank you. We won't be stopping long. Just a quick word with Mrs Maxwell and we'll get out from under foot,' Sander said. He had been tempted. A cup of something hot would have gone down very well

13

in this ice-box of a room and it would have got the chatty Mrs Checksfield out of the way for a time but he did not want to be caught balancing teacups when Mrs Maxwell did put in an appearance. From across the room he heard Gary Blackman's faint sigh and felt the beginnings of a smile behind his face. He was not the only one who would have welcomed something hot and comforting.

'I'm sure she'll be down in a minute,' Mrs Checksfield said and having exhausted that and the temperature and refreshments looked around the room for another topic.

She was saved the trouble. As if on cue, the door opened and another woman entered. It was the woman from the photograph. Older by some years and perhaps older even more now by virtue of the past few hours. Dark circles already rimmed her eyes and she washed her hands together continuously without being aware of the action. Sander observed both throughout the introductions and the mumbled condolences, always his worst moments. If the man upstairs had already cracked, he thought, then here was another who was not far behind him. Just now, she was on a rigidly-held rein that could give at any moment.

'Sorry to bother you Mrs Maxwell,' he said in a low voice after the preliminaries. 'Just a few questions and we'll get out of your way.'

They would be a waste of time, he knew, but they had to be asked. There was always the odd chance of something. The reason that Mark Maxwell had been where he had been at the time; the possibility that someone had said something that had given him a hint of the crime to come without him actually being aware of it; the chance that he had friends who might have been involved; dross that had to be cleared out of the way before the investigation could really get under way.

'Tell me,' he began. 'We've established that your son worked in Blatchford Street, have you any idea what he might be doing outside the bank in Castle Road at that time of the day?'

Mrs Maxwell looked at him dully and a sick travesty of something like a smile pulled at her lips while a note of disbelieving, near-hysteria crept into her one word reply. 'Sausages.'

'Sausages?' Sander echoed.

She nodded and the look about her lips disappeared and her voice took on a dead note as though repeating something that had been gone over and over in her mind. 'Sausages. We like the kind they sell at Mann's in Castle Road and what with his father being ill and the weather what it is Mark offered to pop down there and get them in his lunch break. He was like that – a good boy.'

Sander nodded back and a little sigh oozed out of him. He should have got used to these mad quirks which sometimes made the difference between life and death by now, but he never had. Bloody sausages. He sighed again then ploughed on. The gentle, probing questions followed one after the other. Sander was good at his job and at the end of them he knew what he had known all along. Mark Maxwell had been just a normal, clean-living lad; a bit sports mad with a bit of an eye for the girls and unlucky enough to have been outside a bank when four armed men had burst out threatening people with brandished weapons that had triggered off an instinctive reaction to have a go in him.

'Well that's about it Mrs Maxwell,' he said finally. 'I really am sorry that we had to bother you but we must get these odd bits and pieces cleaned up you know.'

'Of course.'

The woman's voice was so dead that Sander felt compelled to try to inject something into it. 'He was a brave lad,' he said. 'You can be proud of that.'

'He'd have done what he thought was his duty,' she replied and her dull eyes wandered to the picture on the shelf. 'That's his father's training. He always taught the boys that they must do their duty whatever it was.'

Sander's eyes followed hers and he felt a quick stab of pity tinged with a regretful anger at the man upstairs who had bred in his son something that would lead to his death and now lay supine letting this woman carry the burden alone. But then who was he to judge? How would he react if someone appeared and told him that Brian or Reg had been killed? 'Er – yes.'

There was another of those awkward pauses while everyone seemed to edge nearer the door then, apropos of nothing, Mrs Maxwell said suddenly and clearly 'We'll miss him – terribly.'

Sergeant Blackman who had been affected more than he cared to admit while silently taking notes felt suddenly compelled to add his morsel of comfort. 'Well at least you have the others,' he said nodding towards the photographs on the shelf.

Sander saw the extra pain in Mrs Maxwell's eyes and the quick alarm in Mrs Checksfield's then felt the sudden silence that was like a solid weight. It grew until it seemed that the room could take no more then Mrs Maxwell said with a quiet dignity that was more affecting than any outburst 'Kath was killed in a car accident about three years ago and Rob in Northern Ireland at the beginning of last year.'

Sergeant Blackman's face flamed while another flame, a flame of anger, shot through Sander. Gary and his bloody big mouth. Then it died in quick contrition. There was no way that he could have known – either of them could have known – and it was something that he might just as easily have said himself. But Christ, what a situation. He groped for appropriate words in another oppressive silence-then was saved by the bell.

It cut through the quiet house and jerked everyone from the spell of thought upon them. Mrs Maxwell relapsed into her previous deadness, Mrs Checksfield shot from the room in obvious relief while Sander and Blackman went through those vague, shuffling movements of those about to take their leave without quite knowing how to.

They were still performing them when the door opened and framed the man there, Mrs Checksfield bobbing up nosily behind one wide shoulder. He was a big, dark man in his mid-fifties dressed in immaculately-pressed flannels, dark blazer, white shirt and military-looking tie. A big, ornate, regimental badge was woven into the pocket of the blazer. Even without the near-uniform, the man would have looked like the accepted view of a soldier. He held himself unconsciously erect and there was a look of authority stamped on his big-nosed face. It was another of those faces Sander had grown to be wary of. This one was used to having its own way; to being listened to when it spoke; to acting first, thinking later and perhaps explaining never.

He raked Sander and Blackman with a quick hard glance then moved to Mrs Maxwell, his arms held wide. 'Margaret. Oh Margaret. I came as soon as I heard. God, I'm sorry love.'

Mrs Maxwell went into his arms and stayed there for a few quiet moments. He rocked her gently, a pained look on his face as he gazed down at her bent head tucked into his shoulder. The look took on a touch of belligerence when it lifted from her and fastened on the two policemen.

After a while, she drew back from him. There was a touch of moisture about her eyes now but a little more life in her face. 'Thank you for coming Harry,' she said quietly. 'I needed someone.'

'Tom?' he queried, looking down on her.

She shook her head and that travesty of a smile came again. 'He's upstairs. Like a dead man, hearing nothing, seeing nothing. You know how rough he was before this. This has finished him.'

'Perhaps I can get through to him. I'll have a word later,' the man said thickly then half-turned so that he was facing Sander and Blackman, one arm still around the woman's shoulder. 'And these?'

'Oh these gentlemen are police officers. Inspector – er and Sergeant – mm. They were asking about Mark.'

'Sander and Blackman,' Sander supplied.

The man nodded curtly. 'I'm Harry Chapman. Margaret's brother.' His dark eyes got a little hotter. 'Was there really a need for questions at this time?'

'Oh it hasn't been any trouble Harry,' Mrs Maxwell cut in a little hurriedly as though she was well aware of her brother's nature. 'And they've been very good – really. They were just going when you arrived but I've remembered that I meant to ask them about...' She paused then tripped over the words. 'The, er, funeral arrangements.'

'I'll see to all that,' Chapman said instantly. 'Look, you go up with Tom again and I'll sort things out and come up later. All right?'

Mrs Maxwell looked from him to the policeman and then back again. 'Yes,' she said dully. 'Perhaps that would be best.' She nodded as though agreeing with herself. 'Yes. Inspector, Sergeant, thank you for coming,' she carried on then hesitated for a moment. Chapman turned her towards the door with a gentle arm and then she moved on through it leaving a very silent room behind her.

Chapman watched her retreating back for a moment with that same pained expression then lost it as he squared his shoulders and turned to face the others. Mrs Checksfield was the first to receive his attention. 'I think she could do with a nice cup of tea don't you Mrs Checksfield? I know I could.' It was a lot nearer an order than a request.

Mrs Checksfield bobbed her head and went from the room at a bit more than her normal speed.

Chapman looked at Sander. 'Well?'

Sander felt his own shoulders square in spite of himself. He too was a man of authority and did not relish the tone that he was wont to use being fired at him first. 'Well what?'

From the sidelines, Blackman stroked his top lip to mask a faint grin. Both men would have resented the idea but from where he stood they looked oddly alike and it was nice to see the Old Man go on the defensive for once.

'What about the funeral arrangements?' Chapman asked.

'There shouldn't be any undue bother. Of course there will have to be a P.M. and a Coroner's hearing but that's all fairly straightforward. Your funeral director will know how to handle the situation, he'll have done so before with accidents and that sort of thing. Leave it to him. He's the expert,' Sander said flatly and then checked slightly as though suddenly hearing the bark which had crept into his voice. 'If you do run into any difficulty let me know and I'll do what I can to help,' he finished in an entirely different tone.

Chapman recognised the olive branch and nodded curtly, only partially accepting, then the hurt behind his hard face got to him again. 'What a bloody business,' he rasped. 'And to happen to a boy like that. The sort of boy I'd have been glad to call a son of my own. Gunned down in an open street at midday by a bunch of thugs. God, they do what they like these days. I'd liked to have had them under me a few years ago. I'd have straightened the buggers.'

Sander gratefully took the avenue away from the main subject and looked at the badge on the pocket. 'Army man eh?'

'For most of my life. Until a few years ago that is. A C.S.M.,' Chapman supplied. For a moment, he looked as though he might enlarge on the subject but then swung back on the tack Sander wanted to avoid. 'We knew how to treat this sort of rubbish there. Out here in civvy street it's nothing but mollycoddling and bloody social workers from what I can see of it.' He paused fractionally, looked directly at Sander and said what Sander knew he would have to say eventually. 'And your lot are not much better. Half the time you don't even bother to check the louts who grow up into these sort of villains. Too bloody busy chasing motorists and getting people to blow into silly plastic bags and such like.'

It was a slur that Sander had shrugged off

many times but today it seemed to bite a little deeper. 'It's all part of the same job Mr Chapman, routine procedure that has to be followed through,' he said stiffly.

'Like the routine of upsetting a bereaved mother a bit more when you could be out looking for her son's killers,' Chapman rapped back.

It was all wrong. And Sander knew it was all wrong before the words were half out of his mouth. But then the whole afternoon had been all wrong. Over the top. The death of a decent young man; the broken mother and the father lying stunned upstairs; the revelation of the triple tragedy that had struck this household and now this mouthy martinet with his stock answers to a social malady which no police force on its own could hope to cope with. 'We know where to look for them,' he snapped.

Chapman's mouth popped open slightly. 'You know who did it?'

Sander saw the expression, and that on Blackman's face, cursed his lapse into normal, human reaction and went back to being a policeman. 'We have certain lines of enquiry to pursue.'

'Oh, that old stuff,' Chapman sniffed then checked and peered into Sander's face. 'But you do damned well know, don't you?'

'Like I said sir, just certain lines of enquiry. And speaking of that, it's about time we got on with them. Good day Mr Chapman. Sergeant.' He nodded abruptly then went past Chapman with a stiffness which should have delighted the ex-sergeant major in the man.

Blackman paused long enough to note the queer, assessing expression that came over Chapman's face then dismissed it from his mind and followed Sander out.

Sander slumped into the car seat, lit the cigarette he had been longing for and pulled at it savagely.

Blackman slid behind the wheel alongside him and looked at his heavy, set face thoughtfully. It was probably the wrong moment but if there was a rocket to come he might just as well get it out of the way now. 'I dropped a bit of a clanger in there, didn't I,' he offered.

'Not your fault,' Sander grunted. 'There was no way we could have known that they've had all the bad luck in the world.'

Blackman nodded gratefully and, eased himself, set out to put a little salve on Sander. 'That brother's a right irritant and all, eh?'

Sander was half inclined to quick agreement then bit on the inclination. 'You can't blame him. He's hurt and angry and can do nothing about either. I know the feeling.' He pulled on the cigarette again then said savagely; 'That bastard Owen.'

Blackman stiffened a little and peered across at him. 'You putting him in the frame for this one?'

'Who else? It's got his M.O. all over it.'

Blackman wrinkled his nose doubtfully. 'There's Bowyer – or some mob might have skipped down the motorway from the Met and paid us a quick visit.'

'No.' Sander shook his head. 'We'd almost certainly have got a whisper of some sort about that, the locals don't take kindly to foreigners taking their pickings. Bowyer? No, I don't think so. This is Owen, I can feel it in my water. It's got all his earmarks, certain knowledge of what's there then sheer, bloody, brutal ruthlessness in getting at it. Owen.'

'Do you reckon we stand chances of nailing him?'

'Yeah, two.' Sander ground his cigarette out viciously. 'A slim one and no bloody chance at all. It will have the other Owen hallmark as well – damned good cover. He'll have spent the day with a couple of so-called reputable citizens who haven't been caught yet. Tooty Adkins will have been in Majorca – or someone with his passport has. He's probably on his way out there to swop it back again now. Hawkins will have been to a wedding or a christening or a funeral with that damned great family of his and have taken Big Charlie Tooke with him and they'll all remember them vividly because they were the life and soul of the party. Yes, we've got great chances.'

'What about Fred Dew, their wheelman?'

'Oh, Fred will have spent the day alone working in that corrugated iron sewer he calls his garage just to even things out and make it all look a bit more normal. A big brain our Ivor Owen.' He slumped a little more in the seat, took out another cigarette, put it between his lips and then withdrew it and looked at it disgustedly. 'And I'm supposed to be cutting down – fat chance.' He carried on toying with the paper tube for a moment then said almost to himself. 'If ever I was tempted to fit someone up then Owen would be the boy I'd choose.'

Sergeant Blackman's eyes widened slightly. Sander's hatred of the system of picking a known criminal to fit a crime and then making sure that some sort of the evidence was available to prove it was as well known as his feelings about victims. Of a different generation and breed, to Blackman, the system made sense. He would have been happy to nail someone like Owen with even an indecent exposure charge if he could make it stick, true or false. 'There's plenty on the books that would suit him,' he offered tentatively and hopefully.

Sander was silent, tempted for a fraction of a second, then he jammed the cigarette in his mouth and said round it. 'Don't be bloody stupid.'

'Just kidding governor.' Blackman managed a weak grin.

'Yeah, I know,' Sander said casually but each man knew that the other was lying.

There was another silence then Sander said; 'Come on then, let's go and see what Grimm's fairy tale he's cooked up this time.' The memory of the interview just passed popped back into his mind and he added. 'And it better be good because I intend to have the bugger for this one if it takes me a couple of years.'

2

Police Sergeant Philip Bowdery rested his elbows on the bar of the British Legion Social Club and contemplated his world through the remains of a pint of keg bitter in front of him. It had a distinctly rosy hue. This was the first night of a long-deferred seven days leave; he had convinced his wife Mabel that there was no point in taking any sort of holiday at this time of the year and, barring flood, earthquake or sudden revolution, he was his own man for a week to come. The three pints which had preceded the one in front of him added appreciably to the rosiness of the prospect so that he was full of gas and good will as a bulky figure loomed up beside him and a voice said; 'Hello Phil. Haven't seen you in here for a few weeks.'

He focused his eyes on Harry Chapman's big frame and then grinned recognition. 'Oh hello Harry.'

'Going to have one with me?'

Bowdery looked at the near-empty glass in

front of him. 'You can put a head on that if you like.'

Chapman nodded and called the order and then with full glasses both men toasted each other and drank deeply then Bowdery put down his half-empty glass and harked back to the beginning of the conversation.

'No, I haven't been in here much, too damned busy.'

'No rest for the wicked eh?'

'No rest because of the wicked,' Bowdery paraphrased and thought that it was rather good then something about it jogged his memory. God, yes. That business at the bank in Castle Road today. That had been Tom Maxwell's boy and Harry was Tom's brother-in-law. He half-turned to face Chapman and said gravely 'I was damned sorry to hear about your nephew today Harry. A nasty business.'

'A cow of a business,' Chapman answered quietly.

'How's old Tom and his missus taking it?'

'Rough Phil – very rough.'

'Yeah, must be a real blow – especially on top of everything else they've had.' He shook his head sadly. 'I don't know what it's coming to. There seems to be more of these nutters around every day and they always seem to hit those who least deserve it.'

'I'd give them nutters if I had them in a guard-room for ten minutes,' Chapman said grimly. 'We knew how to handle them there didn't we Phil?'

The last time that Bowdery had been in a guardroom, he had been a defaulter himself but he nodded quick agreement. 'Too bloody right.'

Chapman's voice took on a slightly odd note. A note that Bowdery might have detected when behind his desk and fully alert. 'I was talking to your Mr Sander about it this afternoon.'

'Jack Sander? He's a good bloke. We did beat work together years ago.'

'That a fact? He confided that he knew who the villains were, but I don't know. Probably just shooting me a load of bull to cheer me up a bit.'

Bowdery took another pull at his glass, leaving very little in it and shook his head. 'Oh I shouldn't think so, he don't go in for a lot of bull, Jack Sander. If he says he knows – he knows.'

'Oh come on Phil, all you blokes love to pretend to a bit of know-how.' The note in Chapman's voice deepened to near-craftiness. 'You'll be telling me next that you know who did it.'

'I could make a bloody good guess,' Bowdery shot back.

'All right, let's hear it.'

For a second, Bowdery hesitated but his professional competence was being questioned and anyway, this was the club and this was old Harry, one of the boys. He leaned over confidentially. 'Well it's a matter of method, you see Harry. All these villains have got a way of doing things and you get to know them. Now with this job there's only two mobs around here who'll go in for that sort of thing. One's Barney Bowyer's crowd and the other's run by a bastard named Ivor Owen.'

'And who's your best bet for this?' Chapman asked quietly.

'For my money, Owen. Bowyer's hard but he tries to keep away from too much violence. One of his lot might have clubbed your boy out of the way but I can't really see him blasting him out like this lot did. No, I reckon Owen.'

Chapman's voice was a little lower. 'So you should be able to get hold of him pretty quickly?'

Bowdery sucked in his breath and then blew it out slowly. 'Well I don't know about that, my old Harry. Knowing is one thing, proving it's another. We get a lot of that in our game old son.'

'So the sods could walk scot-free?' The voice was almost a whisper now.

It finally got through to Bowdery and he peered at Chapman's face doubtfully. He had a vague feeling that he had done this all wrong; that he had said too much and that something was going on under his nose that he could not quite put a finger on. 'Oh no boy, we'll get them – eventually,' he said with too much conviction and then sheered away from the subject. 'Come on drink up, it's my shout. Harry. Hey Harry. Are you going to have another?'

The words finally got through to Chapman who had gone into a near-trance of thought. 'Eh? Oh sure.' He drained his glass, set it down on the bar and then almost visibly composed his face to normal. 'Not a bad drop of beer tonight. It was off last week you know. Right old hoo-ha about it.'

'Yeah, so I heard. I bumped into Billy Steele and he was telling me about it.' Bowdery called for two more drinks and then began to delve deeply into the mysteries of beer keeping. He was very relieved that things were back to normal but he could not quite shake off the feeling he had felt and a lot of the gloss was gone from his evening.

PART TWO

Effect

3

It was hot and sticky; the rolled stocking-mask covering his coal-black hair was a tight band around his forehead and the gear lever jammed uncomfortably against his right shoulder but Ivor Owen kept his eye glued to the hole that had been punched in the outer skin of the transit van as he crouched cramped in the nearside, foot-well of the driver's cab.

The discomfort was a necessity. It was essential that the driver of the security van saw only an apparently-empty, beat up old wreck as he came along the concrete drive that led to the small factory – and this one had to go right. They needed the money. The pickings from the Castle Road bank job at the end of last year had looked good on paper but there had been a lot of hot, new notes to be traded at discount prices and even the biggest sums had a way of looking not quite so impressive when they were split among five.

Since that time, there had been nothing. That bastard Sander had seen to that. He had been on Owen's back like a dead weight.

It had needed a lot of patience and cunning and authority to wait him out but Owen had all of these and had known that, with the pressure that the police were under, Sander would have to call off sooner or later. He had not reckoned on it stretching into nearly eight months though. But they were back in business now and it looked good. He flexed his eyelid against the strain for a moment then applied his eye back to the hole. Very good. A near-perfect set up. Almost a cul-de-sac at the quiet end of the factory estate; a goods-inwards entrance which was not quite big enough to allow the security van inside and the take all in one nice, easily-portable box.

There was some movement behind him which gently rocked the van and he turned his head irritably. 'Sit still you fidgety bastards,' he growled.

The van immediately rocked again as everyone shifted and took up a new position.

Fred Dew, young, lean and eager, crouched behind the driving seat ready to slip round at a moment's notice. Tooty Adkins, fair, effeminate-looking but as hard and as dangerous as the sawn-off shotgun he held limply in his slim fingers. Poised at the rear doors, Den Hawkins, short, stocky, with a deceptively humorous, nutcracker face and the ape-like figure of Big Charlie Tooke, both carrying pick-axe handles. No shooter for Big Charlie today, Owen had decided. Not after last time. That had been the cause of the trouble that had put Sander on their backs. And so bloody unnecessary. Charlie could easily have belted that kid off or even given him one barrel in the legs had he wanted to make really sure. But no, not Charlie. A nutter. A useful nutter at times but a liability in the long run. Perhaps when this was all over it might be worth while looking round for a replacement. Owen would see. It was not that he had any sort of conscience about the death of a young man, just the pointless trouble which accompanied the death.

The thoughts chased away as he leaned closer to his spy hole and his fingers tightened on the shotgun he was holding. 'Here they come,' he said quietly.

The inside of the van was suddenly charged with extra, suppressed tension.

The security van drove quietly up the concrete road and drifted to a halt outside the factory. No one came out to meet them. That tallied with the information Owen had. There were valuables to be protected inside as well as out and the place did not throw open its doors all that easily.

For a few seconds, the van remained parked and silent, the driver peering through his screen up the road, checking the old Transit then he got out cautiously and stood by his cab door, his attention still riveted on the van.

'We've got a bloody eagle-eye,' Owen whispered. 'I'll castrate the first cowson that moves.' One rock of the van now and the guard would be back into his cab and screaming down the inter-com like a maniac.

For an endless, spine-tingling minute, the guard stood and stared at the van then he slipped out a truncheon and hefted it in his hands thoughtfully.

Owen tensed even more, convinced in his mind that the guard would come forward and check his suspicions, then the man turned and walked alongside the van then went out of sight behind the rear. 'Right,'

Owen said hoarsely.

Fred Dew slipped behind the wheel and the engine he had lovingly mothered for a week or more purred into life almost silently at the first touch of the starter; Adkins, Hawkins and Tooke crowded towards the rear of the van and swung open the doors on their well-oiled hinges while Owen himself straightened from his cramped spot and moved behind Dew and craned his neck for a view of the kerbside of the van. When something appeared there, they would go. It was the essence of his plan that the security boys had a nice, uninterrupted view of nothing but safety as they unloaded their cargo.

A dark shoulder appeared followed by a section of blue helmet.

'Go,' he screamed then turned and lurched towards the rear of the van.

Acrid smoke poured from the tyres as they spun and fought for a grip on the concrete then the van bulleted forward, whipped round the security truck and came to a screaming halt. Adkins, Tooke and Hawkins jumped from the van and hit the road almost in the same motion.

Owen, his brain ice-cool as it always was on these occasions stood half-in and half-out the back of the van and registered the scene. His first impression was that they had come too far. There was a twenty foot gap between them and the security van and the guards were using the time it was taking the three raiders to cross it to make for the factory, dragging a rope-handled box between them. He cursed Dew silently and then cursed again as one of the guards turned and swung his club at the advancing men and they instinctively checked and then made for him in a body. The stupid gets. And what the hell was Tooty doing with his bloody shooter. Christ, he should have given it to Big Charlie after all. There they all were, mixing it like a bunch of street yobs while that other bastard dragged a fortune away from them.

He whipped up his shotgun, rested his arms on the top of the open door and took careful aim at the back of the guard who had continued to drag the box towards the factory and the door that had now slid open revealing a cluster of staring, wide-eyed faces.

The gun boomed. The guard released the box, seemed to run forward for a moment then pitched to the ground with a thud, the back of his uniform a blue tatter that was rapidly changing colour.

The gun boomed again and the cluster of white faces disappeared abruptly and the door began to close as Owen bawled at the struggling knot. 'Never mind him for Christ's sake. Get that bloody box.'

The guard finally went down amid a welter of blows. Big Charlie continued to stand over him while Hawkins and Adkin scurried towards the box and Owen automatically broke the gun and jacked two fresh shells into the chambers.

Then it happened.

For a moment, Owen could not believe his ears or his eyes but that dry, staccato clacking was the sound of a machine gun and they were flying bullets that were whining off the concrete between the two raiders and the box. He stared at the factory for a moment in amazement. They might make hush-hush electrical equipment in there but surely to God they were not guarded by bloody machine guns? His mind steadied itself and rejected the idea and he swung his head to gaze at the far side of the road. There was a linked, wire fence backed by a scrubby hedge of untidy privet and from behind that he caught a flicker of movement – something coloured – the top of a bright crash helmet.

He saw it, was still amazed, but then his

ice-cold mind took over again. If someone was there, then someone was there. The box was still the paramount objective. He turned back to it, saw Adkin and Hawkins crouching near it and bellowed; 'Get that box and come on.'

Hawkins remained crouched but Adkin hesitated for a moment then made a dash for the box, grabbed at it with his free hand and started to drag it nearer the van.

The machine gun rattled briefly. Adkin reared up, his head arched back, jerked in time with the rattle then he fell forward over the box in a limp heap.

It was the signal for a concerted rush by Hawkins and Big Charlie to the fragile shelter of the open, van door.

'What the bloody hell's going on?' Hawkins mouthed through the mesh of his mask.

'Get the box,' Owen rapped.

'Sod the box. Somebody's bloody shooting at us.'

'I know that you clown,' Owen raged. 'Get the box. I'll cover you.' He popped over the top of the door and let go with one barrel in the general direction of the hedge. 'Go on – go – now.'

There was a murderous authority in his

voice and the two men nerved themselves for a frantic dash but before they could move, five answering slugs tore their way through the outermost side of the door in a slanting, wicked line. As one, they hurled themselves past Owen's braced legs into the back of the van.

'Get out of here for Christ's sake Fred,' Hawkins howled at Dew in the driving seat.

Owen ducked back into the van and glared at the men sprawled on the floor. 'Get back out there and get that box,' he said in a voice that was cracking with frustrated rage while the gun in his hand swung over them menacingly.

'There's a bloody maniac out there,' Hawkins argued.

'There's a fortune out there.'

'Then you go and bloody get it,' Hawkins defied from his prone position.

For a moment there was a terrible, pregnant silence in the van as the two men on the floor stared up into the gun barrel controlled by Owen's quivering finger while Fred Dew, twisted in his seat watching all three with doubt etched in every line of his tense frame.

Three more jacketed bullets laced through the side of the van.

They were decisive. 'Fred,' Hawkins screeched and Dew twisted in his seat and let in the clutch and took off with a jerk that closed the rear doors with a tinny clatter.

Owen fought for balance, caught it then let his back slide down the side of the van until he was squatting on the floor. He ripped off the stocking mask and stared morosely at the gun in his lap. He still could not understand what had happened and could not bend his mind to grapple for an explanation. That would come later. For the moment, it was too full of frustrated, killing rage.

There was complete silence after the departure of the van then, from the far side of the hedge came the thumps of a kick starter followed by the putt-putt-putt of a small, motor-cycle engine. It revved for a moment then took off and slowly faded into the distance.

The sound seemed to reach out to the two prone guards. The one who had been shot stirred slightly and began to moan softly. The other pulled himself up painfully until on all fours, his head swinging between his shoulders like a sick dog. Slowly, he lifted his battered and bloody face and gazed

44

dully at the dead body of Adkin sprawled across the all-important box and at the bloody form of his partner behind that. He had vague thoughts about why the box was still there and what had happened but nothing came of them.

The doors in the factory slid wide and men began to run to him from there and, it seemed, from everywhere. He let himself back into a prone position wearily and stopped thinking of anything for the moment.

4

Inspector Sander was too long in the tooth to go charging into anything without some knowledge of what was going on so he parked his car on the outskirts of the welter of police vehicles around and threaded his way through them on foot, nodded to a couple of constables lounging within reach of their radios and then paused behind one car to view the scene in front of him.

His quick eye took in everything. The men taking notes and measurements; the men searching the ground alongside the road and the general urgency of all their movements. Most of all he took in the chalk-marked shapes on the road, the browny-looking stains within them and the earnestly-bent heads of the Chief Inspector and Superintendent from Regional. Big brass and a big job. His lips twitched with satisfaction. He had been right to obey his instincts and survey things first. There was little profit in standing in front of two men like they were without knowing what he was talking about.

He carried on with his inspection until he found the leather-jacketed figure of Sergeant Blackman talking to a uniformed Inspector then sidled round the edge of the group to join them.

'John.'

Police Inspector John Berry nodded down from his beanpole, six foot three while his thin face took on a mocking grin. 'Hello Jack. You took your time getting here. Been having a nice rest somewhere?'

'You try telling someone like old Cademan that you've got urgent business elsewhere when you're chief witness for the prosecution in a case he's trying and see how you get on,' Sander grunted sourly and turned to Blackman. 'What have we got Gary?'

Sergeant Blackman pushed his fingers through his hair and waved the notebook in his other hand a little vaguely. 'Quite honestly, I don't know governor.'

Sander caught the note in his voice and the slight bewilderment on his face and fell back into routine. 'All right then, let's start at the top. What happened first?'

Blackman took a breath. 'Well someone tried to knock over a security van delivering to that factory there.'

He looked like plunging straight on but

Sander forced him onto routine. 'How many men?'

'Four heavies and a driver.' Blackman fell in with Sander's direction. 'Two armed. Twelve bores it seems.'

'That's nice. What were they after?'

'Platinum. The place makes some sort of electronic gear for rockets and missiles and such like and uses the stuff for points and contacts. It's a bit hush-hush so they send the stuff out in small, plain vans. Hence their smallish entrance and hence the security van parking out here.'

'I see. Tailor-made to be knocked over wasn't it? How much of the stuff was there?'

'Ten kilos in one wooden box.'

'Value?'

Blackman consulted his notebook. 'Well it's going at about two hundred and twenty quid a troy ounce so a kilo would be about...'

'Never mind the maths lesson and stick to English,' Sander sniffed. 'What's it worth?'

'About a hundred thousand chief.'

Sander pursed his lips. 'Well that would pay for someone's summer holidays. Were we notified it was on the move?' Blackman shook his head and Sander lifted his eyes to look at the heavens. 'Will they never learn?'

he asked them plaintively. 'All right, then what?'

'The mob jumped the guards between the van and the plant and had their hands on the box.' Blackman paused and took another breath.

'And then?' Sander snapped impatiently.

'And then someone opened up on them with a sub machine gun governor – at least, that's what it sounds and looks like.' Blackman looked a little apologetic.

'Do bloody what?'

Inspector Berry grinned again and dangled a plastic bag containing spent cartridges in front of Sander's face. 'That's what it looks like Jack. My lads found these on the other side of that hedge. Seventeen in all.'

Sander gazed at the shell cases for a moment while he adjusted his mind to the impossible. 'And this is confirmed?'

Blackman nodded. 'As good as. We've got those. Witnesses from the factory said that it sounded like a machine gun and we've got one dead villain with three slugs in his chest.'

'Known?'

'Our old friend Tooty Adkin,' Berry supplied.

This time, Sander's mind moved faster. The number of the raiders, the method, and Tooty Adkin. 'Owen,' he said shortly.

'Could be,' Berry agreed.

'It bloody is,' Sander affirmed with grim satisfaction. 'And this time I'll have him.' He enjoyed the prospect in silence for a moment then went back to the immediate business. 'So this character drove off Owen's lot, gunned down Adkin, and then what – made a grab for the box himself I suppose?'

Blackman looked apologetic again. 'No chief, he just skipped. On a motor bike it seems. John's lads found tyre tracks on the other side of the hedge, one of the witnesses at the factory says he saw the top of a crash helmet bobbing about during the shooting and a couple think they heard a bike start up afterwards.'

'And he didn't even make a try for it?'

'Apparently not. Just shot it out, then moved on.'

'Well I'm damned,' Sander said slowly and made a mental apology to Blackman at the same time for having reservations about the bewilderment he had seen on his face. He was bewildered himself. But he was too good a policeman to spend his time chasing intangibles when he had some hard facts under his hand to go on for now. There was Owen and his connection with the affair and that was a good start in anyone's book. 'Well, I had better go and make myself visible,' he grunted. 'Hang about until I find out what juicy little plum our lords and masters have got for us.' He started away, then checked. 'How are the guards?'

'One's pretty badly peppered in the back,' Blackman told him. 'But the range wasn't too close, thank God. He's lost a lot of blood but he should be OK. The other got the usual pick handle treatment. Broken nose, some teeth gone and that sort of thing. He'll live. Neither was up to talking.'

'Someone with them?'

'One of my lads with each,' Berry told him.

Sander gave him a long, level look. 'It would be nice to know what they say when they're able,' he said casually. 'Just as soon as anyone else knows, that is.'

Berry grinned again then gave him the slightest nod and a slow, heavy wink.

Sander grinned back then turned on his heel and skirted the parked cars once more.

'Sir,' Sander said as he came up to Super-intendent Colin Unwin, then he nodded and said; 'Dave,' to Chief Inspector David Tripp.

'Ah, Inspector,' Unwin said heartily as though he had been waiting for such a pleasure all day.

Tripp merely inclined his massive head and said: 'Jack.'

It was very typical of both, Sander thought. For the bland Unwin, he had little time. Too much the politician, the public-relations career man for his taste. Tripp was another matter entirely. As hard as nails and as blunt as a blow from a hammer and shrewd enough to realise that the same bluntness and hardness which had carried him this far was a bar to him going any further. A realisation which did nothing to help his already-craggy nature.

'Sorry I'm a bit late,' Sander offered. 'Held up in court, I'm afraid.'

'Oh yes. Let me see, what was it?' from Unwin.

'The Bird case,' Tripp supplied. 'What did he get?'

'Two years – suspended,' Sander told him.

'Jesus Christ,' Tripp exploded. 'How long do they think that we are going to go on catching them while they pat them on the head, tell them they're naughty boys and send them on their merry way. Who was the judge?'

'Cademan.'

'Silly old sod.'

The conversation was taking a turn which did not suit Unwin at all. 'Well that isn't really the point at the moment, is it gentlemen,' he cut in smoothly then switched his glance to Sander. 'A weird one Inspector.'

'It is that sir.'

'You filled in on it?' Tripp asked penetratingly.

'All we've got up until now – yes,' Sander answered confidently and got a lot of inner satisfaction from the quick look of grudging admiration tinged with a touch of regret which flickered across Tripp's face.

'Any ideas?' Unwin carried on.

'About the shooting, no. For the initial raid, it's got to be Owen.'

'You've got Owen on the brain,' Tripp grunted.

'Maybe, but this sort of operation and Tooty Adkin left behind as a memento – that's Owen. Tooty never works with anyone else. He's been with Owen since he graduated from Borstal.'

'Hmm.' Unwin pursed his lips thoughtfully. 'You're probably right Inspector, but is he the main objective? We might have a chance at him on an attempted which technically failed. The real point is that we have a murder. An unusual, but nevertheless, cold blooded murder.'

'One must lead us some way towards the other, sir.'

'Yes, that is true.' Unwin nodded gravely and let the two men see that he was giving the matter deep thought. 'Very well inspector. In view of your – er – local knowledge, I should like you to concentrate on the raid angle. You will report directly to Mr Tripp here. The whole thing will of course be entirely under my overall control.'

'Yes sir,' Sander said brightly and kept his tight grin well behind his face. Definitely under your control sir. A case like this was good for some coverage in almost every big daily in the country – probably a nice, juicy T.V. interview thrown in for good measure. Unwin wasn't the man to pass up something like that. Definitely under your control sir. He caught Tripp's hard, knowing glance and carried on smoothly. 'I should like to have a team go over the staff of that factory. They seem to have run a pretty quiet operation and Owen got his information from somewhere.'

'Yes, I agree Inspector.'

'There's always the security people them-selves,' Tripp put in dourly.

'Well we could move on to them afterwards,' Sander offered brightly.

'You seem to think I've got spare men growing out of my bloody ears,' Tripp grunted.

'We all have these manning problems Mr Tripp.' Unwin was full of manly resignation. 'We'll just have to do the best we can. I think this case warrants it.'

'I entirely agree sir,' Sander agreed unctuously. 'I had better get myself into action right away. Wasted enough time today.'

He received a nod of commendation from Unwin, weathered another knowing glare from Tripp and marched blithely away. His mood matched his step. He had a good solid bite at Mr Ivor Owen at last. That his attitude was all wrong, he knew. The human being in him kept pointing out that a man had died violently but the policeman in him could not get too excited at the thought of a double-dyed villain like Tooty Adkin resting in a chilled box with a tag tied to his toe.

'What's our bit then?' Sergeant Blackman asked as he tooled the car away from the press of police vehicles.

'We get the raid side of the investigation,' Sander said happily. 'In other words – Owen.'

'You reckon him for it then?'

'With Adkin involved – grow up lad.'

'What do you think to the other bit – the shooting?'

'I hadn't given it a lot of thought,' Sander admitted honestly.

'It's interesting though, isn't it?' Blackman negotiated a bend a little too fast and checked his speed. 'Weird, but interesting.'

'I suppose so.'

A little exasperation crept over Blackman's face. He did not have Sander's single-minded view of Owen and the policeman in him was intrigued by the other aspect of the case. 'I was wondering about a hi-jack,' he offered, determined to stay on the subject.

Sander sighed slightly then adjusted his mind to oblige Blackman's insistence. 'One man, on a popper-bike. I can't see that. And if it was, why didn't he make a move for the box when he had driven off Owen and co?'

'Perhaps it wasn't just one. Witnesses say that one of the raiders fired back. Perhaps he hit the other one?'

'So now you've got two men on a popper-bike, plus the bullion they hoped to get – some hi-jack. They're clued up enough to know about the raid, clued up enough to be armed with a machine gun, and they use transport like that? Do me a favour Gary.'

'Perhaps there was only one man then and he got hit. Perhaps...' Blackman checked as, his mind not on the road, he hit another bend too fast.

'And perhaps Unwin will ask me to handle the press side of the case for him,' Sander snorted irritably. 'Look lad, just stop trying to get us killed and leave the theories to the big brains. Our job is Owen. Just get us to him in one piece.'

Blackman stared fixedly at the road in front of him in a sulky silence and Sander tried to take his mind back to his original thoughts. Somehow, they did not quite come. Damn Gary and his theorising. But he was right. It was interesting – and bloody weird.

5

The booking-office of Owen's hire-car company was plastic floored, panel walled and chrome finished. It looked clean efficient and business-like and Sander paused for a moment and wondered yet again at the mentality of a man like Owen. He had brains, drive and initiative and yet could see nothing but a profit-making front in this potentially, very successful business. The lure of the quick ten thousand was always infinitely more attractive than the prospect of the long-term twenty thousand. It was something he would never understand.

Owen did both cabbing and self hire and a waiting driver lounged in one of the chairs flanking the wall while an old-looking man presided over a smart counter at the end of the room. Behind him, a two-way radio occasionally erupted into garbled life.

With Blackman at his heels, Sander strode up the room and made to skirt the counter, heading for the padded door behind. He had made enough visits to Owen in the past to know the geography of the place.

'Excuse me sir.' The old man moved sharply enough, despite a limp, to block Sander's progress. 'I'm afraid you can't go in there.'

Sander checked and looked the man over closely. Close up, he was not as old as he had first thought. Mid-fifties, with a face which was seamed with experience, not all good. It rang a bell somewhere in Sander's memory and at the same time he registered the man's respectful stance and the careful politeness of his words. They all added up to one thing in his mind. An old lag. Someone to whom it was second nature to stand partly at attention and put a lot of respect in his tone when confronted by authority.

He took out his identity card and passed it under the man's nose. 'See that dad?'

The man nodded, his light eyes suddenly wary.

'Know what it is?'

'Yes – sir.'

'Well that gives me the authority to go through anything I damned please in this place so move it over.'

The man moved respectfully aside.

Sander carried on past then checked and turned back. 'Do I know you dad?' His inability to place the face irked his trained mind.

'I don't think so sir.'

'What's your name?'

'Munson. Tom Munson.'

'Mm.' The name meant nothing. 'Been here long Munson?'

'Just over three months, sir.'

'Local?'

'No. From London originally.'

Sander let it go. They often had descriptions and photographs circulated by the Met. Perhaps that was where he had seen the face in the dim, distant past. He half-turned then checked again. He might still glean something. 'Were you on duty here this morning Munson?'

'No sir, I don't come on till one, then I go straight through to midnight.'

'Long hours.'

Munson smiled faintly. 'You can't be choosy at my age sir.'

'Or with your background, eh?' Sander probed.

The seamed face went dead. 'Sir?'

Sander studied the lack of expression for a moment then sighed slightly. 'Never mind. Let it ride.' He turned and carried on through the padded door.

Behind the door stretched a lengthy, dark passage with even darker corridors running off to the left and the right. Sander ignored them and went straight along the passage to another padded door at the end. He went through that with the same lack of ceremony he had used on the first.

Owen was seated behind an ornate desk. He was dressed in an immaculate, dark, business suit. Not a hair was out of place on his dark head and his blue eyes registered only a mild curiosity. Sander felt a little tug of alarm behind his sternly-composed face.

'Hello Mr Sander. Come right in, don't bother about knocking or anything like that.' Owen's voice was just another thing about the man which grated on Sander. He might have the dark hair and blue eyes which betrayed his Celtic ancestry but his voice was the flat, adenoidal twang of the midland slum into which he had been born. Just now, it also had a ring of mockery and confidence.

'Never mind the funny bits,' Sander grated. 'This isn't a social call.'

'Oh. Disappointed again,' Owen mocked. 'Well Mr Sander, if it isn't social, what is it?'

'Where have you been today?' Sander asked flatly.

Owen considered quietly for a moment before answering. It was a cool, deliberate provocation. 'Well now Mr Sander, that sounds a bit like it could be the beginning of something heavy. Perhaps I ought to have my brief here? After all, there's two of you and only one of me if it comes down to what I am supposed to have said.' His hand drifted towards the telephone on the desk.

Sander shrugged casually. 'Fine with me. Tell him to come straight on down to the nick – that's where you'll be.'

The wandering hand stilled and the voice lost a little of its mockery. 'For what?'

'Questioning. If you won't answer a few simple questions here then I've got good grounds for thinking you've something to hide and good grounds for taking you in. Suit yourself.'

Owen locked eyes with him for a moment then spread his hands and relaxed back in his chair. 'You're a hard man Mr Sander. Ok, what was it you wanted to know?'

'I'm not going to stand here repeating myself like a bloody parrot to amuse you.'

'Oh yeah. I remember. Where have I been today. Well it's no great mystery. I spent the morning with Nick Bayliss arguing about what he charges me for servicing my fleet and trying to thrash out a cheap rate for doing the lot. After that, I came straight back here. Haven't been out of the place since.'

'What time did you get back?'

'About one. No, it would be dead on one. The old boy on the counter outside was coming on duty and he's never late.'

'And what time did you leave Bayliss?'

Owen shrugged. 'Oh I don't know – exactly. How long does it take to get from there to here – ten minutes? I suppose I left about ten minutes or quarter to one.'

Sander computed and figured behind a stony face. Owen was covered for the time of the raid if Bayliss confirmed his story – and Bayliss would. A character not unlike Owen himself, he owned a large and flourishing garage but could never resist a quick, extra profit. He was clever like Owen too. All the suspicion in the world but no form. On the face of it, a respectable citizen. He felt the beginning of frustration build within him. He had calculated wrongly. Figured that after such a fiasco, even a character like Owen would have panicked a little, left a few ragged edges. He should have known better. Owen had recovered and was back in the driving seat, even to this little bit of gilding with that business with the old man out front. He bit on his disappointment and ploughed on.

'Anyone see you with Bayliss?'

Owen gave it some thought, started to shake his head, then checked. It was great acting. 'Oh yes. His secretary brought us some coffee a little after eleven. She'd probably remember me.'

Sander had a quick vision of the sort of girl a man like Bayliss would have for a secretary. 'I'll bet she would,' he grunted sourly. 'All right, what about the rest of your mob?'

'Mob, Mr Sander?' Owen was nothing but injured innocence.

'Adkin, Hawkins, Dew and Tooke.'

'Friends, Mr Sander. Friends.'

'So we play silly games. Friends then. Where are they?'

Owen shrugged. 'I don't know. We don't live in each other's laps. The only one I'm fairly sure about is Tooty. He was on about popping over to France for a bit of a holiday. If I know him, he never got beyond Paris. You know what he's like.'

'I know what he's like now,' Sander said grimly. 'A corpse. He's dead.'

Owen fell back in the chair and let his mouth drop open. It was still worthy of an

Oscar. 'You're pulling my pisser Mr Sander.'

'I wouldn't touch any part of you with a barge pole,' Sander told him.

Owen recovered enough to shake his head bemusedly. 'What was it – an accident of some sort?'

Sander looked at him stonily for a long moment then jerked his head at Sergeant Blackman. There was silence while he left the room and then Sander turned back to Owen. 'All right. Let's stop sodding about. It's just you and me. No witnesses, no nothing. Now I know you were on that raid this morning and I know you were there when Tooty copped it.'

'Mr Sander, I...'

'Shut up and listen. Now you may find it hard to believe, but this time I'm not really after you,' Sander lied. 'What I am interested in is the nutcase with a machine gun. He's the one who's important at the moment. So let's forget about the raid and concentrate on who could have known about it and who's got it in for you enough to want to spike you. You help us on that and the rest is water under the bridge.'

It was a good try and Sander put enough false sincerity in his voice to make it believable. For a moment, the quick, hard

65

flash in Owen's eyes said that he too had been asking the same questions for the past hours, but then they were all innocence again. 'I'm sorry Mr Sander, but I don't know what you're talking about – honest. What raid? And what's Tooty got to do with a man with a machine gun?'

Sander sighed inwardly. He had flopped – badly. 'All right Owen, we'll play it your way – for now. But I'll have you my son. Believe me, sooner or later, I – shall – have – you.'

Owen's smile was thin. It barely masked the quick rage within him. He was a man who had grown used to making threats on his own account. 'Pity we didn't get my brief in on this Inspector. He could have made a nice little harassment charge out of that.'

The hands hanging at Sander's sides balled into fists as he looked at the sneer on Owen's face then he took hold of himself. A clever bastard this Owen. He had almost reversed the positions. He was the one who was supposed to get rattled. 'Yes – a pity. I'll try to do better next time   and there will be a next time.'

He turned to go and Owen was out of his chair in a flash. 'I'll see you out Mr Sander,' he said civilly.

In spite of himself, Sander felt a tinge of

professional appreciation. The bugger didn't miss a trick.

Back in the booking hall, he paused by Tom Munson, acutely aware of Owen looming behind him.

'You say you came on duty at one?'

'That's right sir?'

'See anybody?'

Munson looked puzzled. 'No sir.'

Sander stiffened. 'No one?'

'Well – no one in particular. Mr Owen was getting out of his car in the yard and when I got round here my relief, Ted Stacy was looking out of the window for me, but no one else.'

It was cleverly done and Sander felt his temper rising again as he looked at the lined face before him. 'Mr Owen dressed as he is now?'

The face went from him to Owen behind him, then back to him again with that former puzzled air. 'Why yes sir – just the same as he is every day.'

Owen's air of triumph was almost something solid as it wafted across to him. He turned and marched down the room without another word. Blackman caught the set of his stiff back and hurried after him quickly.

Outside, in the car, he lit his inevitable cigarette.

'We didn't do too well on that one,' Blackman hazarded, in spite of the set face.

'I blew the bloody thing,' Sander muttered savagely. 'Underestimated the perisher.'

'What now then governor?'

'Now? Back to the old plod game, I suppose. Drop me off at Bayliss's place and I'll try to knock a few holes in his story. You had better start trying to dig out Hawkins and Big Charlie. It shouldn't be hard. If Owen's prepared them as well as he's done everything else, they won't be hiding.'

'Right. Want me to pick you up later?'

'No. I could be any time and you don't know where you'll be led to. I'll buzz in for a panda.'

Blackman nodded and looked at the set face again. 'We might get lucky with Hawkins or Tooke,' he offered consolingly.

'Yeah – round about the time I draw my pension,' Sander grunted.

Blackman gave up the hopeless task and let the clutch in.

From inside the booking-hall, Owen watched the car glide away and a hard grin curled his lips. He felt better than he had done since the chaos of the morning and he turned the grin onto Tom Munson, coupled with a nod of approval. The old man had done well. Owen had not really needed his story. He had only arrived a little later than anticipated after his time-table had been thrown out, but it was nice to have all the loose ends tied up and he had felt in need of a little extra assurance when everything else had gone so wrong. The old boy had supplied that little extra very nicely and Owen had been pleasantly surprised at the speed at which he had caught on and his easy agreement to back him. It was nice to know that he had someone else around to rely on.

'You did great pop,' he said heartily.

Munson smiled wanly. 'Glad to help, Mr Owen.'

'You won't regret it. I know how to look after my friends.'

'No need for that Mr Owen. I've got no reason to help the law anyway.'

'Has anybody?' Owen asked and cackled at his own joke.

After a perceptible pause, Munson contributed another wan grin and a nod of agreement.

6

Inspector Sander sat at his desk and felt sorry for himself. Things had started badly twenty-four hours ago and not got any better since. The interview with Bayliss had been a frustrating replica of the one with Owen and his secretary, a gum-chewing blonde with a figure like Venus and a voice like a band-saw had proved equally unshakable. Just to add to that, Blackman had discovered that Hawkins and Big Charlie Tooke were away on a short holiday together. A caravan site at Sheppey, too many of their friends said. Blackman had gone down there this morning but with that much preparation having gone into the alibi, Sander knew what to expect from that.

That just left Fred Dew. Sander had pulled him in and put on his rough man act. He might have been auditioning for a part in a play for all the effect it had made on Dew. Fred had gaped at him round a wet, brown, hand-rolled cigarette and then remembered that he had been at a used-car auction twenty miles away when all the excitement was going on. Someone certainly had. Fred had two receipts and a phone call revealed that a Frederick Dew had bid for and obtained two old bangers. A tall, thin young man? Mm, most probably. Firm identification? No, sorry. With two hundred faces there, the auctioneer was doing well to remember him at all.

Sander had released him with all the vile threats he could think of hanging over him. The curses salved his drooping spirits a little but had no effect on Fred at all.

The final depressants had come within the last hour. Records had nothing at all on a Thomas Munson and Detective Chief Inspector Tripp had wanted a word with him.

Tripp had quite a few words. None of them complimentary. They were given added emphasis by the fact that he was also up a very blind alley. The shot-up van had been discovered, empty and as clean as a whistle. It was with that forensic lot now but he did not expect much from that. The tyre tracks behind the hedge had been identified but did not narrow the field much. First estimates thought there might be a couple of hundred thousand in use in the country.

The check at the factory was bringing up nothing and both guards had recovered enough to tell their stories but, 'were about as much use as tits on a bullock,' to use Tripp's poetic phrase. To round off, he more than hinted that he had the same feelings about Detective Inspector Sander.

Things were not going at all well.

The office door opened and Sander looked long enough at Sergeant Blackman's face to know that things had not got any better.

'No joy, eh?'

'It was a nice ride down. The countryside's lovely at this time of the year.'

'I'm not in the mood for the patter,' Sander told him sourly. 'What did you get?'

Blackman composed his face and took out his notebook and consulted it as though he did not already know it by heart. 'Hawkins and his wife went away last week-end for a break in their caravan. Because they like him so much, they took Big Charlie with them. By an odd coincidence, the caravan next door is occupied by Hawkins' aunt and uncle and two female cousins. The blonde one is supposed to be the light of Charlie's life at the moment. A lot of coy giggling there. Actually she's about as charming and coy as a shotgun.'

'I told you I wasn't in the mood,' Sander growled.

'Sorry gov. Anyway, yesterday the whole crew, aunts, uncles and everything went for a swim in the morning. The water was very cold. In the afternoon they all played some sort of football. They all laughed and made so much noise at the sight of Big Charlie falling about that half the camp site can verify the fact. It's all very pat. You've got to give that Owen credit. He's tied up all the ends very nicely.'

It did Sander no good at all to be reminded of something that was itching at him badly enough anyway. 'It's not credit I'm going to give him – and stop building him up into some sort of superman. He's just a hard-nosed villain who's a bit worse than most, and don't forget it.'

'Yes gov. Sorry again gov.' Blackman relapsed into a diplomatic silence.

Sander brooded at the desk for a long moment. When it came down to it, Gary was right. The bastard was clever. That it was true did not make it any more palatable but it did make him relent a little and when he looked at Blackman again, the bite had gone from his glance and his voice. 'Any impressions?'

Blackman frowned thoughtfully. 'There's a couple of points. The first is, I don't think they've got a clue as to who or what hit them. The feigned astonishment at the raid and Tooty's death was not all acting. They were really shaken by what happened and very much in the dark about why and who. The other thing that might be worth looking at was something Hawkins said. He had an idea that...'

'Hello slaves,' a big voice interrupted.

Both men stared at the overweight, slightly-breathless figure lounging against the silently-opened door – then both men grinned.

Everyone grinned at Brian Gander, inevitably nick-named Goosey, and the head of forensic in the county. The three-chinned, rubicund face radiated a fat geniality which inspired a friendly, but faintly patronising, reply. It was a face which was worth a fortune to him in the witness box as an expert and had trapped many a fledgling barrister who had considered it easy meat only to find that behind it lurked a razor-sharp mind and a man who was master of his trade.

'Hello Brian,' Sander said and his voice was brighter than it had been all day. He and Gander had a long-standing friendship based on liking and mutual respect. 'What are you doing out in the backwoods?'

'Slumming,' Gander wheezed and heaved his bulk across the room to ease it into a chair by Sander's desk. 'I had to come and deliver my report directly to the all-highest so I thought I'd look in and see how the lower orders are getting on.' he favoured Sander with another grin and Blackman with a heavy wink.

'Come off it,' Sander chuckled. 'You don't give a damn how we are, you just couldn't resist getting your big nose directly into something as odd and as juicy as a machine gun attack.'

'You may have something there. But let's be accurate if we're going to insult each other. It was a machine pistol actually. An M.P. Forty, thirty-two shot, German, circa nineteen forty-three, if the ammo is anything to go by.'

'German,' Blackman said. 'Blimey, don't tell me we've got an imported, urban terrorist to deal with?'

Gander shook his chins negatively. 'I shouldn't think so sergeant. There were a lot of these about over here at one time. They break down easily and men brought them home as souvenirs after the war. There's a lot less now of course, but this one is definitely still operational.'

'Some souvenir,' Blackman said.

'True, but then people are like that. Look at the things that were handed in during the amnesties. Christ, we even had an anti-tank gun right here in this county and I've seen a pair of cannon-shells polished and standing at each end of a mantelpiece as ornaments and the damned things were live and ready to go.'

'So now we're looking for a mad, souvenir collector?'

'You wish,' Sander cut in. 'No, this will be the old, old story. Some squaddy brings home a lethal weapon to remind him of the good times he had. It's all right with him, he thinks, he knows about it and he's never going to use it. Then some yob breaks into his house one night and the next thing you know we either have a looney kid terrorising the district or we've got one more weapon on the open market to be used by some nutter sooner or later – typical.'

'That's about the strength of it,' Gander agreed.

'And apart from this very technical difference between a machine gun and a machine pistol, has your brilliant section come up with anything else?' Sander asked him.

He shook his head and then grinned. 'I could waffle on a bit and blind you with science, but when you get down to it – no.'

'As usual – you're a big help,' Sander said.

'We can only do the best with the little we're given. Oh, there is one thing though. I think your boy is a real expert.'

Sander looked at him keenly. 'How do you work that out?'

'The way he finished the job off. Machine pistols are not the easiest things in the world to be accurate with and though the bullet patterns on the van and the roadway show the usual, lacing effect, your man knew what he was doing when it came to the crunch. As nice a little grouping as you could wish to see in Adkin's chest. Any one of them could have killed him.'

'That's a comforting thought,' Sander mused and brooded quietly for a moment.

'I thought it might cheer you up,' Gander agreed and hoisted his body from the chair. 'Well I can't sit here doing your thinking for you all day.' He started for the door. 'See you Jack.'

'Yeah,' Sander grunted, still thoughtful, then shook his head. 'Oh, and thanks for the info.'

'That's all right. It would have filtered down to you lower echelon people sooner or later anyway.'

'I like you too,' Sander sniffed. 'But just a sec. What about the van, anything on that?'

'Nicked a fortnight ago. Engine tuned to perfection and as clean as a newly-dusted, baby's bottom inside,' Gander said, then made his face look a little grave. 'Three nice sets of prints on the outside though.'

Sander's head came up. 'Yes?'

Gander nodded slowly and then his fat grin popped back. 'They belong to kids between about eight and eleven judging by the size of them.'

'Bugger off,' Sander told him shortly.

Gander bowed gravely then oozed out of the room.

'Silly perisher,' Sander called after him then turned a partial grin on Sergeant Blackman. 'A nut case.'

Blackman nodded. Both, he might be, but at least he had put Sander in a better mood. 'Think he's right about that expert theory?'

'Quite likely. He's not often wrong.'

'So someone could have put a notice out on Tooty and called him in to do the job?'

'It's an idea.'

'It is that. And it ties in with what I was

saying about Hawkins.'

'Hawkins? Oh yes, you were telling me when Goosey came in. What was it?'

'Well Hawkins said something about it being a wonder that Tooty hadn't been knocked off ages ago, the way he lived. Then he reminded me about all the bother there was last year when Danny Stenson came out and found Tooty shacked up with his old woman – remember?'

'I do now, but I had forgotten. It's true enough, I suppose. You never knew what bed you were going to find Tooty in next and he put a lot of noses out of joint. Doesn't make the hit man very bright though, does it?'

'How's that governor?'

'Well he could have slipped in, done a quiet hatchet job on Tooty and slipped out again and I for one wouldn't have broken out in a muck sweat looking for him – and that goes for half the jacks in this county as well. This way, he's got all the publicity in the world and even the lollypop men looking for him.'

'Mm, that's so, but then a lot of them are like that aren't they? The bigger the show, the bigger the name, and the bigger the price next time out.'

Sander nodded thoughtfully. It made sense

that some exhibitionist killer might have picked that way to do it and there was little point in looking for rationality in a man who murdered for a living. They came in all shapes and mentalities. 'You could be right. Ok, start looking round to find out where Tooty was parking his Y fronts before this and put the word out that we want to know about any strange face with a reputation who might have been in the patch lately.'

'Right governor.' Blackman liked the thought that his idea had been taken up. 'Something might come up and, at least, it's another angle to work from.'

'True,' Sander agreed and then a little of his former mood began to seep back. 'And we need another angle lad – we really do.'

7

'You stupid, great, red-necked berk,' Owen raged down into Big Charlie Tooke's upturned face.

Big Charlie's hands curled under the chair he was sitting on while his face mottled angrily. He was not used to being spoken to like that but though he could give Owen six inches in height and a stone and a half in weight, he sat and took it. He had seen Owen perform in the past and, even with the courage of stupidity and brute strength, he wanted no part of something like that.

On opposing ends of Owen's desk, Den Hawkins and Fred Dew looked oddly similar as Dew rolled a cigarette with a fixed air of concentration and Hawkins stared at the desk top as though he had never seen it before. They too had seen Owen in a rage and they were strictly neutral at the moment.

'You want the inside of your bloody skull looked at,' Owen carried on. 'I told you to ferret around not take on Bowyer's lot on your todd and then stick two of them in dock, you pratt.'

'They asked for it. They came looking for me,' Big Charlie mumbled defensively.

'Oh I don't doubt that,' Owen sneered. 'But what did you do to set them off – walk straight up and ask them if they were the ones who had screwed us and then offer to beat them to a pulp if they didn't turn it in? I can just imagine you trying to make quiet enquiries.'

Big Charlie got a little bolder. 'What's the duff anyway? They were Bowyers.'

'The duff is, thickhead, that we don't know for sure and we don't want to go off half cocked until we do.'

'They were still Bowyer's – and it's got to be Bowyer what done it,' Big Charlie argued.

'Oh, so you're doing the thinking and all now are you? So why Bowyer then? Why did he want to tuck us up?'

''Cause he knew that we'd had a little tickle or two at his territory during that bad patch while we was waiting for this last job,' Big Charlie offered conclusively.

'I know he knew,' Owen sneered. 'And he knew why and that it was only temporary and that we were only picking up peanuts. He was prepared to swallow that providing we didn't get too flash and even if we had been, he'd have wanted to come and talk about it first. I know Bowyer. That's his way. He don't duck any bother but he doesn't go out of his way to find it.'

'I still think...' Big Charlie began.

'Think. You couldn't think if you had a brain transplant. You make me sick.' The scope of his anger increased. 'The whole bloody lot of you make me sick. You're all supposed to be wide – have your ears to the ground, and what have you come up with after four weeks sniffing around – flaming nothing. You're all useless.'

There was a little silence then Den Hawkins lifted his eyes from the table and looked at Owen with a hint of anger of his own. In spite of his lack of size and merry-looking face, he was the hardest man of the trio when it came to the crunch and was not prepared to take the sort of tongue-lashing Big Charlie had been subjected to.

'Leave it out Ivor,' he said with a little snap in his voice. 'That sort of chat don't help nothing.'

There was another silence. A charged silence this time as Owen picked up the hint of challenge in Hawkins' tone. He considered it for a moment then said quietly: 'You telling me what I can or can't say now Den?' The calmness in his voice was suddenly a lot more dangerous than his rage had been.

Hawkins shifted his position a little as though to get more room but kept his eyes on Owen. There was a deliberate lack of challenge in those eyes but they held very steady. 'No Ivor – no way. I'm just saying that it don't do any good to kick our arses about something we can't do nothing about – any of us. We've all tried but nobody knows nothing. There's no buzzes, no whispers – nothing.'

Big Charlie grunted agreement and, after a pause, Fred Dew weighed in with a nod of approval.

Owen's gaze had not left Hawkins but he noted the signs from the others and his mind slotted into its normal, cold appreciation of a situation. There could be trouble here. They did not really want it. But there could be if he pushed it too hard. He should have remembered that they were as jumpy as he was himself. Slowly, he forced away his external anger. He did not enjoy the experience and someday would extract payment for it. Owen had a long memory when it came to recalling slights. But this was not the time.

'But we should have come up with something by now,' he offered in a flat tone. 'There's got to be something somewhere.'

'Sure Ivor – you're right – we'll just have to keep pushing.' Hawkins' own tone and his face were both conciliatory as he accepted the return to a status quo and a lot of the charged tension went out of the room. 'Mind you, I still think that it could have been somebody who just had it in for Tooty alone.'

'Like who?' Owen sniffed. 'We know this manor. Who's around capable of pulling a caper like that?'

'So they could have put out a notice on Tooty.'

Owen shook his head. 'I still can't see it. No pro would go to the trouble to put on that performance when he could have done it so much easier. No, this was aimed at me – us. Someone wanted to screw us just at the moment we thought we'd got it made. Tooty was incidental. It could have been anyone who went for that box who bought it.'

It was Hawkins turn to shake his head. He had a native intelligence and a lot of animal cunning but this notion of psychological pressure coupled with physical violence was a little beyond him. 'That's pushing it a bit, isn't it boss,' he said doubtfully.

'I still reckon that bleeder Bowyer for it,' Big Charlie cut in before Owen could answer.

In spite of his earlier resolve, anger seeped back into Owen. 'If you come out with Bowyer again I'll...'

A light tap on the office door checked him.

There was another tap and then the door opened to reveal Tom Munson balancing a tray piled with canned beer. 'Here's the wallop you asked for Mr Owen.'

Owen blinked for a moment, then nodded. 'Oh yeah, I'd forgot I asked you pop. Bring it in and stick it on the table.'

Munson limped across the room and began to transfer the beer to the desk. His actions were inept and one can tipped over and rolled towards Big Charlie, threatening to land on his lap.

In his tight mental state, the sudden movement made him jump. 'Watch it, for Christ's sake,' he rasped as he grabbed for the can.

Munson visibly cringed. 'Sorry Mr Tooke.'

The attitude and the apology only goaded a man with Big Charlie's mentality. 'Sorry, you silly old perisher. Sorry don't help nothing.'

'Knock it off,' Owen rapped.

'Sorry Mr Owen,' Munson said to him.

Owen made his voice light. 'That's all right pop. Just set them down and blow. Take no notice of him.'

Munson fumbled the remainder of the cans onto the desk and limped out hurriedly.

Big Charlie scowled at the door which closed behind him, pulled at the ring of the beer can and muttered. 'Silly old sod.'

Owen bent a hard glance on him. He was getting his fill of Big Charlie this evening. 'Lay off him,' he ordered in a tight voice. 'He did me a turn when the filth were creeping round here after the raid.' He paused and added quietly: 'And I don't forget them either.'

It was all beyond Big Charlie. 'Eh?'

'Forget it – dummy. Just leave him alone.'

The anger which had never really left him stirred again in Big Charlie, Owen was at him again. 'He gives me the creeps,' he rumbled. 'He's always around under your feet with his yes sirring, no sirring, three bloody bags fulling, just like a bloody zombie.'

Hawkins saw the coming storm in Owen's face and made haste to cut it off. They had just got over one blow. 'Too much porridge,' he said lightly.

This too eluded Big Charlie. 'Eh?' he said again.

Hawkins grinned, glad of the chance to pull Charlie from Owen's orbit. 'Oh come on Charlie. Even you can't be that thick. You've been there my old son. Now where have you seen poor old geezers like him with all the crap kicked out of them?'

It came to Charlie slowly. 'Oh – in stir – Christ yes.'

'There's a clever boy,' Hawkins mocked.

'All the more reason for him giving me the bloody creeps then,' Big Charlie muttered.

Anger clouded Owen's face again but Hawkins cut it off once more. 'Anyway, we didn't come here to talk about him this evening, did we.'

He had hoped to steer to neutral ground but Big Charlie was not to be denied. 'Too bloody right. What we ought to be talking about is what we're going to do.'

'Do?' Owen frowned. 'We are going to carry on trying to find out who wants to screw us, that's what we're going to do.'

'No, I didn't mean that.' Charlie shook his head. 'I mean what are we going to do to pull in some lolly. I'm right skint.'

That charge came back into the room

again suddenly. Dew got an even blanker face, pulled at his moth-eaten cigarette and then took it from his mouth and examined it as though surprised to find that it had been unlit for several minutes: Hawkins lost his trace of humour and leaned back in his chair and folded his arms like a man who had done his best but had now given up; Owen took on a glacial look, his eyes cold, empty glass.

'You mean, pull a caper?' he asked quietly.

'What else?' Big Charlie shrugged.

A muscle popped in Owen's cheek as he bent forward to impress Charlie with his nearness but he kept his voice flat and even. 'Look Charlie, I'll try to get it through to you. We are pulling nothing. Not only have we got the filth watching every move we make but, more important, we still haven't got a clue who it was got at us.'

'So? Does that mean we've got to sit and twiddle our bloody thumbs?'

'Too damned right it does. Can't you see it for Christ's sake? Whoever turned us over last time knew about the job in advance. They knew. Understand? And if they knew about that they could know about anything we get into. Next time they could shop the lot of us if we don't dig them out first. That's the priority Charlie and until we do dig them out, you don't even drop litter on the pavement my son.'

Big Charlie could see some sense in the argument but Owen seemed to have missed the salient point. 'But I'm skint,' he repeated.

Owen's sucked-in breath thinned his nostrils. 'That's got damn all to do with it. Anyway, if you didn't wank your money away on those big cars and bigger birds you go swanning around with, you might have a few bob to fall back on.'

'What I do with my lolly is my business.'

'True.' Owen leaned a little closer. 'But what you do to get it at this time is very much mine Charlie and if you even think about pulling a stunt – I'll top you – and that's a promise.'

Big Charlie saw the fulfilment of that promise in Owen's face then turned his eyes to Dew and Hawkins. All he saw there was blank approval of Owen's words. A baffled rage built up within him. Christ, could nobody see what he was talking about? What was he supposed to do, go bloody hungry or something or creep about poncing like some little yob who had just come into the game? He was Big Charlie Tooke. Somebody. And to be somebody took money.

He opened his mouth to argue and then looked into Owen's face again. Animal awareness suddenly replaced his rage. There was danger here and he needed out. That was first. After that could be seen whether Mr bloody Owen was God or the near relation he seemed to think he was. Craftiness masked his small eyes as he lumbered to his feet.

'All right boss, no need to get stroppy. I get the picture,' he said mildly.

Owen had tensed at his movement, now he studied his face carefully. With anyone else, he could not have accepted the sudden about face, but Big Charlie could never be that subtle, he thought, underestimating the instinct for survival which possessed even an animal like Charlie. 'Ok then,' he said a trifle uncertainly.

'Ok,' Charlie repeated then turned away. 'Anyway, if that's all there is, I'll drift. Got to see one of them big birds you were on about boss.' He grinned placatingly and carried on across the room.

Owen watched his progress, frowning slightly. He was still not sure – but he could buy a bit of time. 'Charlie,' he called.

Big Charlie checked, then turned slowly, his bull-like frame poised for quick action. 'Yeah?'

'If you're that skint, here's a bit to tide you over.' Owen fished out a wad of banknotes and peeled some off. 'Two ton, that should keep you going for a bit.'

Charlie grinned hugely as he accepted the proffered notes. 'Thanks boss, you're a gent. Sorry I was so thick. Well, gotta blow. Bye all.'

He shambled from the room.

Owen continued to regard the space he had vacated as though he were still there, his lips pursed thoughtfully.

Hawkins watched the expression on his face then lit a cigarette and got up to stand beside him. 'Could get dodgy if he gets the bit between his teeth,' he offered quietly.

'Eh?' Owen came out of his thought trance and looked at Hawkins' expression through the cloud of smoke that wreathed it. 'You reckon?'

'I reckon.' Hawkins took another puff and put more smoke around his face. There was none of his habitual merriment now and through the smoke the face looked hard and vicious.

'You think he's shooting the shit then?'

Hawkins shrugged. 'Anybody else, I'd say yeah straight away – with Charlie – who knows? Might be worthwhile thinking about tucking him away somewhere for a bit though. That couple of hundred ain't going to last long – not the way Charlie gets through lolly.' He put more smoke about his face then half-whispered: 'Perhaps even sort of permanently like?'

'I thought you were his oppo?' Owen said, his face expressionless.

'When it comes to a ten year stretch, I got no mates.' Hawkins summed his life philosophy up in a single sentence.

Owen grinned and then shook his head. 'No. It's worth remembering for the future, but not now. The same applies to him as everybody else. We can't take any chances yet – but some day...' He left the promise for the future unspoken.

'And for now?' Hawkins asked.

'For now, we keep tabs on him day and night and if he looks like stepping out of line then, chance or no chance, that's it.'

Hawkins nodded. 'I hope the stupid git realises that.'

'I almost half hope that he doesn't,' Owen murmured.

Hawkins looked at his face, thought how close he had come to falling out with it earlier on and took another long pull at his cigarette.

Big Charlie tramped savagely past the cars parked in Owen's yard, his hands pushed deep into his pockets against the chill which was beginning to creep into the autumn nights. On the far side of the yard, Pat McQuade, the ex-pug hired by Owen to guard the vehicles, came out of his hut, peered across to identify the stamping figure, then waved a greeting.

He got no answering wave. Big Charlie was not in the mood for pleasantries. His mind was too full of the events of the evening. He knew that he had been put down and he knew that he had been frightened and he was a stranger to both experiences. He might push both into the back of his mind but they were still there and the feeling made him vicious and self-pitying.

That bloody Owen with his cold eyes and big ideas. It was all right for him. He had his business to get by on while times were bad. He could afford to hang on and find out. Find out. What the bloody hell was there to find out? It was that berk Bowyer behind everything and that was that. Wait until he got his hands on one of his pratts again. He'd show them. But first things first. He had to find a caper to get in on. That two hundred wouldn't go far. Two bloody hundred. And he had handed it over like it was the crown jewels. Sod Owen – and Hawkins and Dew and all the rest of them.

He reached his car then paused, his band on the gleaming chrome and white cellulose creation. The feel of it lifted his spirits a little. Now this was something. This was Big Charlie Tooke. Owen could sneer all he wanted but you were something in a baby like this. Even the bloody pedestrians passing in front of him while he waited at the lights paused for a quick glance as they scuttled across. Yes, a man who owned one of these was nobody's mug.

He opened the door and slid in behind the wheel, taking immense satisfaction from the quiet click of the closing door and the expensive smell of newish hide that greeted him. Then he leaned forward and started the engine. The big, overhead cam power unit purred into life and Charlie sat and enjoyed the sound of it. Ham-handed and heavy-footed in most things, he made no demands on the motor until the engine had warmed and moved from the automatic choke. Not for him the impatient blip of the throttle and the scream of tortured tyres. The only thing he really cared about in life deserved better treatment than that.

He listened to the engine even out, grunted with satisfaction then gently depressed the clutch pedal. Sensitive as he was to the vehicle, his foot picked up the slight amount of extra pressure needed on the pedal then he heard a faint, metallic tinkle and something dropped between his feet.

He had five seconds. Five seconds to wonder what had fallen; to think about what he would do to those bloody, greasy-handed mechanics who had serviced the car last week if they had mucked anything up; to put the gear shift into neutral and repeat the clutch action to see if the noise reoccurred; to start to...

There was a crump, and a flash, and a blasting force which slammed his big body back into the seat. The trunk only, mainly. From there down, there was not a lot of him left to be thrown anywhere.

8

Sander was past the open cursing stage and had sunken into plain, vile temper as Sergeant Blackman hammered the squad car through the gates of Owen's yard causing the constable who was guarding it to step smartly aside and fling a few well chosen words after it.

He seemed fated to always be somewhere else when anything broke in this Owen affair. It had to be tonight that the informer Sergeant Blackman had unearthed had agreed to a meet. And he had to be one of those shrinking violets who insisted that the venue was some God-forsaken place out in the back of nowhere. And just to cap it all, he had to have proved damned near useless. Oh he knew something. The fact that Big Charlie Tooke had tangled with two of Bowyer's boys in a private gaming club and that they were now tucked away in a nursing home, one with a fractured jaw and the other with a damaged spleen where Big Charlie's size eleven brogues had thumped into him. That had an authentic ring and he knew the names of the men and the location of the home. But the rest was fantasy. The big, gang-war fantasy that the underworld like to come up with from time to time and the comic-paper Sundays lapped up. And it was based on fantasy. Someone had heard; someone knew someone who had seen; someone had been told by someone. The usual mass of chaff with one tiny grain of fact hidden in the middle.

He puffed with annoyance as he flung open the car door and got out. Gary would hear a lot more about this when he had some time later on.

Inspector Berry, who had watched the screeching progress of his car with a twist of wry amusement, moved out of the coned-off, floodlit area around the wrecked vehicle to join him beside the squad car. 'Hello Jack. Lively little turn up eh?'

'Hello John.' Sander's eyes picked out the blackened outline of the wreck. 'Big Charlie?'

'None other – or what's left of him.' Berry nodded to the ambulance parked outside the circle of light.

Sander followed the nod and then frowned. 'You haven't taken him away yet?'

'No. Goosey said he might want a quick

look at him.'

'Goosey? Gander's here?' Sander was surprised and faintly alarmed. The one comforting thought during the mad ride here was that, at least he would arrive before the top brass. Four weeks ago, the woods had been full of eager beavers but as the case had stagnated they had slowly drifted away. Unwin had hummed and hawed about important matters requiring his attention while Tripp had frankly admitted that: 'he had better bloody things to do.' Nominally, they were still in charge but the leg-work and slow, sifting grind was quietly dumped on Sander and those below him.

'He's here all right,' Berry said with a chuckle. 'He was down at the nick on a routine enquiry that had caught his fancy when the news came through. As soon as he heard it was a bombing he got so eager that I thought he was going to hoist me on his back and gallop down here without waiting for a squad car.'

'Anyone else here?' Sander asked – too casually.

Berry chuckled again. 'No – you're safe son.'

Sander gave him a scowl and peered at the floodlit circle. 'Where's Goosey now?'

'He's on the other side of the wreck. As soon as we got here, he wedged that body of his into a pair of overalls and then wedged both into the car. All I've seen of him since is a giant arse sticking out of the door.'

Sander gave him another scowl and moved off towards the car.

Berry shook his head and gave another wry grin. He was glad that he had opted for the uniformed branch. He had never yet seen a detective who, sooner or later, did not get obsessed with some case and lose all his sense of proportion. It must be an occupational disease. He shook his head again and followed Sander's retreating back.

Sander surveyed the taut, great buttocks emerging from the car doorway for a moment then leaned across them and put his head inside the car. 'I know that face,' he said lightly to get a bit of attention.

All he got was a twitch of the buttocks and a definitely irritated mumble so he stepped back to join Berry as he came up.

'Not a pretty sight,' Berry said with another of his grins.

'You're full of them tonight aren't you,' he said sourly. There were times when he wished these uniformed woollies would take things a bit more seriously and this was one of them. This made two weird ones now and the damned thing was getting out of control.

'Just bringing a little light relief to the situation,' Berry answered, unperturbed. He knew Jack Sander and he knew the mood would pass once he got his teeth into the thing.

Something like the same thought filtered through to Sander in the silence which followed. The wasted evening, the late news, the mad ride, the discovery that Gander was already on the spot, they had all combined to distort his judgement and make him snap at anything and he was no good to anyone like that – least of all himself. The analysis was also tinged with a touch of self-interest. He would need the co-operation of John Berry and his lads long before they would need his.

He squared his shoulders mentally and said in an even voice: 'Have you come across anything I ought to know?'

Berry cocked an eyebrow at the change of tone, chanced a smug look then shook his head. 'Nothing much Jack. You've got one long range eye witness but he won't be much help.'

'Who is he?'

'The yard man, Paddy McQuade.'

'McQuade? That rings a bell. Known?'

'He's been in minor bother a few times. Punchy, ex-pro fighter turned minder, bouncer, or anything else that doesn't require an overweight brain. You might have heard of him from time to time.'

'I expect so, but he doesn't really come to mind. He minds this yard for Owen does he?'

'Yes. Evenings only. Apparently Owen gets a lot of bother from beered-up yobs looking for something to go for a joy ride in.' Berry grinned widely. 'Nice to know that he's not immune from them. I don't know which I enjoy most, the thought of Owen being vandalised or the picture of what someone like McQuade might do to the vandals if he caught them.'

'Does your social worker know the kind of thoughts you harbour under that uniform?' Sander asked dryly then looked round into the darkness of the yard. 'Long range, you say?'

'From his hut over there.'

'Hmp. He'll be a big help then. I'll get to him later. What about Owen, I suppose he's his usual mass of quivering nerves?'

'He didn't quite strike me like that. He's

his usual snow-white, simon-pure of course. No idea why it happened. Can't possibly imagine who would want to do away with a charmer like Big Charlie. All the usual rubbish.'

'I'll get to him later as well,' Sander promised grimly then peered at Gander's rear. 'He's taking his time. You don't think he's had a heart attack do you?'

'With the sort of luck we're having lately – yes,' Berry stated with conviction.

As if to prove him wrong, Gander's rotund form twitched violently and then backed out of the ruined car. Sander thought of Berry's 'not a pretty sight' and a grin touched his own lips. Gander deposited some articles on the roof of the car and then turned to face them. His face was flushed with undue colour and he was puffing strongly. Sander's own remark about a heart attack looked to be an imminent possibility. The front of his overalls bore some ominous-looking stains and he pulled a cloth from his pocket and wiped something from his hands which half inclined Sander to turn away. He was not the most squeamish of men but there were some jobs he would not have undertaken for twice his pension. Gander did not appear to be affected by any similar feelings.

He puffed a bit harder and said: 'Bloody modern cars. Built for midgets.'

Sander thought of the size of Big Charlie and shook his head in wonderment.

The movement seemed to attract Gander's attention. 'Hello Jack lad. Well you're coming up with them lately aren't you? This old manor of yours is getting to be the most interesting patch in the county.'

'I'm glad we're pleasing someone,' Sander sniffed and looked beyond Gander to the wreck. 'Find anything? It was a bomb, I take it?'

'No – termites,' Gander chuckled wheezily.

Sander sighed. 'It must be something in the air, the place is full of them tonight.'

'Eh?'

'Bloody comedians,' Sander supplied.

'You're getting old and crotchety Jack my boy. Where's your sense of humour?'

'Over there in that ambulance with what is left of Big Charlie,' Sander told him.

Gander's breeziness died. 'Mm. I suppose you're right. Yes Jack, it was a bomb.'

'Plastic – jelly – something like that?'

'No – nor any of your modern, electronic firing devices. It was a nice, old-fashioned grenade.'

'Grenade?'

104

'Yep.' Gander turned and picked up the articles from the car roof. When he turned back he held a threaded, distorted chunk of metal and a twisted lever in one hand and a piece of wire with a ring holding a split pin in the other. 'Here,' he held out the chunk and the lever. 'There's the base plug, nearly always gets blown out clean, and there's the firing-pin retaining lever.'

'Well I'm damned,' Sander breathed.

'And this was how it was done.' Gander stretched the wire and the ring between his hands. 'Grenade lashed to the steering column, probably close up under the dash where it would not be noticed. This wire down to the clutch pedal. Very neat. The pedal's depressed, the wire pulls out the pin and the retaining lever pops off then down goes the striker, bang goes the detonator, fizz goes the fuse and – bingo – exit one villain. Yes, very neat.'

'You're a genius,' Sander said with a little snap in his voice, annoyed by the professional approval in Gander's. They were all the same, these forensic bods. So wrapped up in their own little world that they seemed to forget that it was human life they were discussing – even the life of someone like Big Charlie Tooke.

'Wait a minute,' Berry came in. 'If that thing operated as soon as the clutch was used, then it had to be put on since the car was parked – in this yard – tonight.'

Gander beamed at him. 'There's clever. We'll make a detective out of you yet John my lad.'

'Over my dead body,' Berry told him. 'I like my own bed for most of the nights of the week too much for that.' He shook his head. 'But who the hell uses grenades for a job like this these days?'

Sander had a quick recollection of Blackman's remark about urban terrorists but pushed the idea aside. This had to be connected to Owen and he was not the man to get mixed up in anything like that – there was too little profit in it. 'I don't know,' he said then switched his eyes across to the hut that Berry had pointed out. 'But that long-range witness of yours begins to take on a bit more importance.' He turned his gaze back to Gander. 'Anything else startling?'

'I don't think so.' Gander shook his head. 'We'll give it a closer going over when we tow it in tomorrow and I'll have a quick look at the remains before I leave tonight, but I don't expect to find anything. I think this lad was a bit too cool to leave anything stupid lying about.'

Sander took up the remark. 'Cool?'

Gander nodded. 'Too right. Figure it out for yourself Jack. I should imagine he had some wire round the grenade already, probably slipped through the serrations under the clip. He couldn't take a chance on disturbing that clip – even this lad. But he still had to wire it to the column and then fiddle about getting the right tension on the trip wire and almost certainly in the dark. For that you've got to be cool. Cool nerved and steady handed.'

Sander's mind went back to the raid and the slaying of Adkin. 'You figure it was the same man who put those shots into Tooty's chest?'

'Like I said Jack,' Gander told him quietly. 'Cool nerved and steady handed.'

Owen stood up behind his desk as Sander came into the office and Sander took a brief moment to study him. There were perhaps the slightest signs of tension about his eyes but perhaps he was imagining even that. No panic. That was Owen's hallmark. Plan, hit, and stay calm enough to pick up all the loose pieces. It was what had kept him a free man for so long.

'Well?' he said.

'Well what, Mr Sander?'

Sander sighed slightly. 'Come on Owen, we're both too wide to play games at this time of the night. Let's hear your cooked up version.'

'Cooked up, Mr Sander?'

'Owen,' Sander warned ominously.

Owen shrugged. 'All right Mr Sander. There's no need to get stroppy. Not much to tell anyway. Big Charlie came here tonight, we chatted for a bit and then he left. A few minutes later I heard a sort of thud and then old man Munson came galloping in here with his eyes hanging out of his head and told me Charlie's car had blown up. That's about it.'

'And you rang the law like a good little citizen?'

'Naturally.'

'Yeah, naturally. What was this chat between you and Charlie about?'

Owen grinned. The truth was always best when it could not hurt. 'He was moaning about being skint, so I lent him some money.'

'Beginning to feel the pinch was he?'

'Sorry Mr Sander?' Owen looked blank.

'Save it for those who might be impressed. What else did you chat about?'

'Oh – odds and ends.'

'Odds and ends like him crippling two of Bowyer's boys perhaps?'

Owen's face remained expressionless but his eyes flickered momentarily. Definitely sharp this bastard Sander, and with a good ear to the ground. 'First I've heard of that Mr Sander.'

'I'll bet,' Sander sniffed, then he checked and sniffed again, deeply. Even to his tobacco-deadened sense of smell there was a rare old fug in here. Cigarettes, beer, and to the best of his knowledge he had never seen Owen smoking – or Big Charlie for that matter. 'Big Charlie the only one in here tonight?' he asked casually.

Again Owen's face was wooden but this time his mind was racing behind it. Sander had been wrong in his initial assumption. Owen could panic. Had panicked slightly and obeyed his instinctive reaction to split the gang as he always did in times of trouble, sending Hawkins and Dew out into the night with instructions to find some cronies who would bear out any story they liked to give. After that, there had barely been time to give the beer cans and some hurried instructions to Tom Munson. McQuade did not matter. Unlike Big Charlie, Hawkins and Dew were

109

not fussy about who had access to their vehicles so had parked them in front of the building giving McQuade no knowledge of their presence. It had been a stupid mistake, he now realised – unnecessary. Unimportant also, perhaps, but it left a chink and he knew the way the law had of ferreting out chinks and levering at them until something more significant appeared. He hoped fervently that the old man had taken in all his hurried words. A lot could depend on him.

'No. Nobody else,' he said blandly.

Sander noted his words, tested the atmosphere again and tucked the discrepancy away in his mind to be used in the future. 'This McQuade character, you had him long?'

'A year or more.'

'And he's in that yard all night?'

'No. He comes on about eight, leaves about twelve. That's the time I'm likely to get trouble from bloody yobs wanting a quick set of wheels.'

'Rough – you should ask for police protection.'

Owen sniffed.

Sander permitted himself a faint grin then said: 'What time did Charlie get here tonight?'

'About seven I think it was.'

'Seven. And McQuade didn't get here until eight you say?'

'I suppose so. I don't clock him in and out. He just tells old man Munson that he's here and that's that. He'd only come in to tell me if he hadn't turned up.'

'And he didn't tonight?'

'No. So?'

'I'm doing the questions,' Sander grunted and went into some thought. That left the car unattended for an hour. But an hour of daylight. Gander had probably been right. It wasn't the sort of job you chanced in daylight in the middle of an open yard. His first radio call had put the time of the explosion at just after nine thirty. And it got dark about eight thirty now. There was another hour. An hour of darkness. But an hour when McQuade should have been watching over things.

He ignored Owen's questioning face, marched to the door, opened it and said to the waiting Blackman: 'Wheel that McQuade in here,' then moved away from the open door and looked at Owen thoughtfully. This wasn't going to be strictly by the book. Witnesses and suspects should be questioned apart but he had the feeling that something was going on here and that he might get more by mixing procedures a bit. He had never been a great one for going by the book anyway.

McQuade was a big man with a heavy head and bunched shoulders. His nose was fairly intact but he had deep scarring around the eyes and he blinked rapidly and often. He was obviously punch-drunk but there was also the stamp of natural brutality and stupidity on his craggy face as he faced Sander suspiciously as though ready to charge at a second's notice.

'All right McQuade, tell me what happened tonight.'

McQuade frowned. 'I already told everybody over and over again.'

Barely a trace of an Irish accent, Sander noted as his lips tightened. Odd how they all came down to a common level of communication. 'Well now tell me.'

'Nuthin' to tell really. I see Charlie Tooke going towards his car and give him a wave. He didn't wave back. He got into the car and a couple of minutes later, it went up – bang.'

'It didn't blow as soon as he got into the car?'

'No, I told you. It was a good couple of minutes.'

'What time did you come on duty tonight McQuade?'

'Usual – 'bout eight.'

'Only about?'

'Well I dunno exackly. Ask old Munson. He's the one what takes notes about the time everyone comes and goes.'

'Is he now? Everyone? That's interesting.' Sander looked at Owen. 'You forgot to mention that.'

Owen shrugged casually. 'Is it important?'

'It could be,' Sander said quietly then turned back to McQuade. 'All right, you were on about eight. Did you see anybody in the yard between then and when the car blew?'

'Couple of drivers come in and dumped their cars.'

'What time?'

'Oh – dunno. Anyway they just went on through the yard to sign off with Munson. He'll know the time.'

'And you didn't see anyone else?'

'No.' McQuade shook his bullet head in the negative then said. 'Except Pop Munson.'

Sander stiffened. 'Munson was in the yard tonight?'

'Yeah.'

'After dark?'

'Mm – yeah.'

Sander looked at Owen again and read the puzzlement on his face. There could be something here. 'Let's have Munson in as well sergeant,' he told Blackman. 'Make it one, big, happy party.'

There was silence until Blackman ushered Munson into the room. He blinked a bit nervously at the faces in there then assumed his usual, half-servile posture.

'I understand you book everyone coming and going?' he asked casually and silkily.

'That's right sir.' Munson nodded. 'To do with the business, that is.'

'Of course. A couple of drivers booked out sometime after eight. Remember them?'

'Bloom and Tucker sir.'

'Remember the times?'

'Oh, Bloom was about eight-fifteen and Tucker close to nine, I think. I could get my book and check exactly for you sir.'

'Later will do.' Sander's voice was still very smooth. 'I also understand that er, you were prowling around the yard tonight?'

Munson looked suddenly alarmed. 'Me sir? No sir.'

'Oh? Funny. McQuade here says that he saw you.'

'But he couldn't. I wasn't...' Munson

114

checked and looked curiously at McQuade. 'Only when I took his coffee out sir.'

'His coffee?' Sander too looked at McQuade and started to curse in his mind.

'Yes sir. I have a bit of a brew up every night and take Paddy a cup out.'

'Yes?' Sander asked McQuade wearily.

'Dat's right.'

'You thick sod,' Owen rasped and Sander mentally thanked him for saving him the trouble.

McQuade blinked from one to the other. 'What's wrong? Yer man asked me who else I'd seen and I told him.'

Sander looked into his face to see if he was being taken on then said quietly: 'Never mind,' and turned back to Munson.

'What time did you take the coffee out?' Munson figured thoughtfully. 'Well it wasn't long after Bloom checked out and well before Tucker came in. I should think about eight-thirty sir. It's somewhere about that time every night, varies a bit depending on how busy I am at the time.'

'Was it dark?'

'Mm. Just coming down sir. But quite dark, I suppose.'

'And did you see anyone or notice anything peculiar out there?'

'Afraid not sir – sorry.'

'All right,' Sander said resignedly. 'You two can go. You had better go with them sergeant and get the names and addresses of those drivers. They might have seen something.' The group started for the door then Sander remembered the smell of smoke. 'Just a minute Munson. What time did Tooke get here?'

Munson considered for a moment. 'I couldn't be dead sure sir, but it would be about seven.'

'Come alone?'

'Why – yes sir.' Munson registered a little surprise.

'And no one came through to the back here all evening?'

The surprise remained. 'No Sir.'

'All right. Go with the sergeant.'

Sander turned from the closing door just in time to catch the smug satisfaction on the face of Owen and the familiar, baffled temper that the man always aroused in him began to build. 'You've got them all well trained,' he rasped sourly.

'Inspector?' Owen's face was bland.

Sander put whitened knuckles on the desk in front of Owen and leaned forward belligerently. 'Never mind the bloody party games. You remember what I told you last time out?'

'Vaguely,' Owen drawled insultingly.

'Well you had better manage a little more than, vaguely. What applied then is even more so now. You and your doings are even less important than ever. It's this maniac that is the real problem and the signs are that it's not going to end here. It must be obvious to even a cocky swine like you now that this lad is after you and yours. You may not like it any more than I do but it's getting so that we are on the same side. So let's have some co-operation. What's going on Owen? Who's after you and why?'

For a moment, the look on Owen's face revealed that he too had been asking the same question in his mind since Munson had burst, wide eyed, through the door. Then it veiled to normalcy and he shrugged. 'Sorry Mr Sander, I just don't know anything.'

'And you wouldn't tell me if you did eh?'

'Why of course I would Inspector.' The amusement in Owen's tone was open and obvious.

Temper grew stronger in Sander but then he put a hard block on it. He must be getting old to let this character continually throw him on the defensive like a rattled man.

'Ok smart boy,' he said casually. 'We'll still play it your way. Come to think of it, might not be a bad idea at that. With any luck it will be your car he gets to tomorrow night. See you – in the mortuary.'

The look on Owen's face lifted his spirits considerably as he left the room.

9

Tripp motioned him to the chair in front of the desk in the borrowed office with a curt jerk of his head and Sander sank into it with the nasty feeling that this had all happened before. Apart from the fact that it was now forty-eight hours since the crime, it was almost a repeat of his experiences of a month past. He had got nowhere; the two drivers had proved to be of no help; forensic had come up with nothing new and now he was about to get his arse chewed off by Detective Chief Inspector Tripp.

There was one minor difference however. He was not exactly in the mood for it this time. He had worked long and hard over the past forty-eight hours and was tired and to his bafflement with Owen and the case had been added a resentment at the way that everyone seemed to have flooded back on the case expecting miracles after having quietly drifted away during the interim period.

'Not much here.' Tripp drummed a thick finger on the papers in front of him.

Sander craned his neck to identify his latest report. 'Not much to put in it yet.'

'No. Not likely to be either, the way we're going on,' Tripp rumbled.

'We're doing the best we can.'

'Hmp. Is that what it is?'

Sander's lips tightened at the tone of Tripp's voice. Here we go. 'D.C.S. been on the phone?' he said nastily.

Tripp caught his tone and his eyes glinted across the desk at him. Battle was joined. 'He has – and he's entitled to the way that people are sitting there letting things slip quietly past them.'

Why the hell don't you say what you mean, Sander thought with rising anger and said flatly: 'What people – what things?'

Tripp's finger drummed again. 'There's a bit here about two of this man Bowyer's people being worked over by the victim.'

Sander frowned. 'Barber and Giles. Yes, I interviewed them. I reckon it as one of these dust ups that breaks out between rival hard cases from time to time. My opinion's in there.'

'But you didn't follow it up.' Tripp leaned forward, put his elbows on the desk, laced his fingers and rested his chin on them.

The attitude looked quietly menacing and

Sander searched his words for the trap. 'Follow it up? With Bowyer do you mean?'

'That's the way it struck me it ought to be done. You obviously don't agree.'

'No – I don't.' Sander's tone gave no ground at all. 'What are we supposing then, some sort of gang war between Bowyer and Owen?'

'You don't put it down as a possibility?'

'I considered it, yes – then rejected it.'

'Oh well, that's the end of that,' Tripp said sarcastically.

Sander took another hold on his temper and leaned forward to emphasise his points. 'Look sir, at the start of this thing, someone said my local knowledge had value. All right, let's use it. We've got two big villains in this patch, Owen and Bowyer, but they're entirely different. Owen's the shark and Bowyer the octopus.'

'Very poetic,' Tripp sneered heavily.

'But apt,' Sander cut back shortly. 'Owen strikes hard on a single job but Bowyer's got a finger in everything. Prostitution, protection, clip joints, porno, and almost anything else you like to think of. Only occasionally does he get involved in a blagging and then it's mainly as a backer. Apart from that, he's strictly non-violent.'

'Well that is nice. So while this er, octopus, doesn't get too rough, you allow him to go his merry way, eh?'

'You know me better than that.' Sander's face flushed and his voice lifted. 'And you know the score. Every patch has got a Bowyer. If I had three times the men and twice the amount of time, I could nail him. Until that day comes, I can only make life difficult for him and wait for him to drop a bad clanger.'

Tripp's eyes grudgingly acknowledged the truth of the statement but he pressed on with his point. 'All right, I was a bit personal – but it's still your opinion that Bowyer isn't involved in a war with Owen?'

The trap was yawning wide again but Sander saw no way to avoid it without loss of face. 'It is.'

Tripp grinned nastily then straightened and passed a piece of paper across the desk. 'Like to have a look at that? The collator picked it up this morning. Good thing some-one's not in blinker's around here.'

Tripp's choice of words burned but Sander kept a wooden face as he accepted the proffered paper. He kept the same wooden face as he read it but his spirits went down a little with each word. He passed it back and looked squarely at Tripp. 'Interesting, but on the face of it it's still a straightforward hit-and-run. There's no evidence there of anything dodgy.'

'Oh come on Jack.' Tripp's face registered impatience. He banged the papers in front of him a little more violently. 'It says here that this Waylett character was Bowyer's right hand – been with him for years – knows more about him than anyone. Do you want me to believe that, in the middle of all this hoo-hah, it's just sheer coincidence that a top lad in what could be the opposing gang just happens to walk under a car late at night?'

'It could be,' Sander defended a little lamely.

'Could be?' Tripp exploded. 'For Christ's sake Jack, take off your blinkers. You've got this thing about Owen and about the whole affair being a local set-to without any outside interference and it's blinded you. You've handled the whole damned thing on a parochial basis without really considering that we could be dealing with imported talent specially brought in. Now haven't you?'

Mentally, Sander had to admit that he had – and still would in spite of this latest development. He had a feeling in his bones that he was right and he had learned to rely on that feeling over a lot of years. 'Maybe I have,' he agreed. 'But I know this patch and I know Bowyer and, most of all, I know Owen. I talked to him the other night and though he wouldn't tell me what time of day it was, I know that he was as much in the dark as we are and he is not the sort to go off half-cocked and start something like this if he's not damned sure he's right.' He leaned forward and thumped the papers on the desk in his own right. 'The bastard's too cold blooded for anything like that.'

'Oh forget the psychology bit for once,' Tripp rapped. 'From now on this is going to be handled the way it should have been from the start. We're getting Criminal Intelligence in, C.R.O., the lot. We're going to have the record of everyone who pulls stunts like this and get the thing down out of the Sherlock Holmes class to a proper business footing.'

Sander groaned inwardly. He had visions of the mountains of paper involved; of the time taken checking and following them up; and of the endless waiting while over-taxed forces outside their area tried to fill the requests for checks on men they could not get to themselves. And, in his mind, it was still damned unnecessary. 'I should imagine that we'll be flooded with candidates who open fire with sub-machine guns and then potter off on motor-bikes and with villains who kill with grenades in this day and age,' he sniffed.

The truth behind the statement touched the practical policeman in Tripp on the raw. That in turn, brought out his rank and authority. 'Don't be so bloody sarcastic – Inspector,' he gritted.

For a moment, the two men glowered at each other across the desk. Sander was the first to take a grip on himself.

'Sorry – sir.'

It took Tripp a little longer. 'Hmp,' he grunted then lowered his gaze and fiddled with the papers on the desk. When he finally looked up, his expression had returned to its normal, heavy composure. 'Anyway, that's the way it's going to be. I want you to make a start by digging into this so-called accident and I want you to lean on this Bowyer and put the fear of Christ into him. We cannot afford any escalation that this might lead to so I want it made very plain to him that if he's got any ideas about taking the next bite, he'll think the bloody roof fell on him. Got that?'

'Yes sir.' There was no heat in Sander's tone but it was very stiff. 'Anything else sir?'

'No,' said Tripp a little wearily and watched Sander get up and leave the room. The weariness spread to his eyes as he noted the stiff back and the firm closing of the door behind it and he sighed lightly. There were times when this job... Oh – bugger it.

'Inspector Sander and Sergeant Blackman to see Mr Bowyer,' Sander told the fluffy, little, blonde receptionist.

The bruising still in him from the interview with Tripp put a bark in his voice and a grim set to his jaw and the little blonde blinked at him anxiously. The look changed a little as she moved on to Gary Blackman's open face and wide shoulders then changed even more as she caught his quick wink. She started a grin; a grin which died a quick death as Sander split his glare between her and Blackman. She gabbled the message into a desk communicator while Blackman assumed an expression of wooden innocence.

In spite of his mood, Sander felt a flicker of amusement behind his face as he waited, looked round the plush offices of Bowyer's Entertainments Limited, and wondered again at the criminal mind. Bowyer was another, even more so than Owen, who could have made a success of almost anything he put his mind to and yet preferred the shady side of life. He wondered too at his own attitude towards Bowyer. He was a villain with a finger in every mucky pie in the area and the policeman in Sander would have given a lot to have put him away for a long, long time – and yet he had never felt the same personal animosity toward the man that cropped up whenever he had dealings with Owen. Perhaps it was because there was at least a touch of humour and humanity about the man? Perhaps it was the veneer of respectability that he at least assumed? Perhaps it was the fact that a constant collection of minor crimes spread over a period and an area did not jar his professional suscepti-bilities as much as the outright violence which erupted from Owen? Perhaps... He gave the thought up and felt his inner grin again. At least it proved that most people were wrong – policemen were human.

His musings were interrupted as a door to the right of the blonde's desk, bearing a plaque which stated, J. Waylett, opened and a man lounged into the reception area.

He was too-smartly dressed, tall, lean, and

with dark good-looks that failed to mask the inherent viciousness in his smooth face. Just now, the face was wearing a mocking grin.

Sander stiffened and had a succession of quick thoughts. The first was reaction dislike. He knew Vince Amato and did not like him one little bit. The acknowledged leader of Bowyer's heavy mob, he was, in Sander's mind, only one step behind a character like Owen – and trying hard to make up that step. The second was surprise. Bowyer was far too smooth usually to advertise the fact that he had muscle like Amato on call especially in the aura of respectability he strove to build around these offices. The third, and lasting thought, was suspicion. If Bowyer felt the need of someone like Amato close at hand, then perhaps there was something in this gang warfare theory after all?

'Hello Mr Sander,' Amato said with barely-concealed mockery in his tone. 'What can I do for you?'

'You can do nothing except lose yourself,' Sander said shortly. 'I'm here to see the shepherd, not the dog.'

Amato's dark eyes heated for a moment, then he got his grin back. 'Very good Mr Sander. You always did have a nice way of putting things.'

'I'm glad you're pleased. Now ring a bell, or do a cartwheel, or whatever else you have to do to get Bowyer.'

'*Mister* Bowyer.' Amato paused insultingly while he casually got out a cigarette. 'Well that might not be too easy. *Mister* Bowyer's a very busy man and can't see every Tom, Dick or Harry who comes busting in here.'

Sander blinked in quick surprise. It was all out of pattern. He was used to some lip from characters like Amato, but only up to a point, and he certainly was not used to being denied access when requested, especially from someone like Bowyer. 'Are you telling me I can't see him?' he asked slowly.

'Well, I don't know now.' Amato lit the cigarette and grinned craftily through the cloud of smoke. 'After all, it ain't as if you've got any God-given right to see anyone any time you want, is it – not unless you got a warrant, that is.'

Sander blinked again. In a way, he supposed, the man was right. It was certainly a moot point. Then rising anger whipped the thoughts from his mind. His voice lifted a notch or two. 'Sonny,' he warned slowly. 'I don't know whether you're on the bottle or have been sucking reefers but I'm going in to see Bowyer and if you as much as let out one more yap I'll run you in so fast your feet won't touch.'

He started towards the door behind the blonde's desk.

Amato stiffened, checked for a moment, then started as though to block him.

Sander felt fresh surprise but he was in the happy position of a man who did not have to bother about the reason for the surprise. 'Gary,' he barked loudly and carried on towards the door.

Gary Blackman, who had been enduring with barely-controlled patience, got a tight smile and moved purposefully towards Amato.

It had all the ingredients of a lively few minutes then a hard voice said: 'What the hell's all the... Oh, hello Inspector.'

'Hello Bowyer.'

'You want to see me?'

'That was the general idea but your pup here seems to have some objections.'

Bowyer cocked his grizzled, grey head at the tone while at the same time his sharp, little blue eyes took in the scene. He was a short man but his blocky shoulders almost filled the doorway in which he stood. He had a tough, square face which was normally softened by inbuilt good humour but just now it looked hard and sharp. 'Vince?' he queried of Amato.

'They were going to just come busting in,' Amato said sullenly. 'I didn't see why they...'

'Forget it.' Bowyer's tone brooked no argument, then he seemed to make a slight effort and softened it. 'Cool it down Vince boy, Mr Sander's welcome here any time, you know that.' He added a grin to the words and then turned it on Sander. 'Come in Mr Sander, come in.'

Sander nodded then paused and said to Blackman: 'You better stay out here Gary in case the natives get restless again. And I don't want to be interrupted while I'm in there – understand?'

Blackman nodded, looked at Amato as though he hoped that he did not understand then perched himself on the edge of the receptionist's desk. He was alternating between giving her a very broad glad eye and sneering at Amato as Sander followed Bowyer into the inner office.

'Sorry about that Mr Sander, take a seat.' Bowyer indicated the chair on one side of his desk and went round to sit at the other.

Sander sank into the chair, shook his head

at the cigar box Bowyer opened in his direction, lit a cigarette of his own and bent a hard glance on him. 'What was all that about?' he asked huffily.

'Eh? Oh Vince. Nothing to worry about Mr Sander. Rush of blood to the head. Newly promoted and all that sort of junk. You know.'

'Newly promoted?' Sander thought of the close-mouthed Waylett who had been Bowyer's right-hand man. 'You don't mean you've moved that loon up into Joe Waylett's place?'

'Well you can't keep young talent down forever.' He paused while his eyes got thoughtful then said pregnantly: 'You know how it is Mr Sander.'

Sander nodded thoughtfully. He did know. He got the picture very well. Tough, young blood, closely in touch with the grass roots and beginning to pressurise the tough old blood that had been at the top perhaps too long. 'Yes, I know,' he said. 'Expensive though.'

'Expensive? How's that?' Bowyer looked puzzled.

'Now you'll have to hire someone else to watch him watching your back.'

Bowyer gave a tough, tight grin. 'I've

looked after my back for quite a few years Mr Sander, I think I can probably manage a few more.' His eyes got thoughtful again. 'I shall miss Joey though. He was a good lad.'

'One of nature's gentlemen,' Sander sniffed.

For a moment, Bowyer's eyes heated up, then he got his grin back. 'Always a joke eh? I take it, it's because of Joey that you're here Mr Sander.'

'You take it right. What's your version of the affair?'

Bowyer shrugged. 'Same as everyone else's I suppose. Joey had had a few – he's been knocking it back a bit lately – he wandered out of the club, half pissed and someone else-probably half pissed as well – whanged into him with a motor. That's it, he was dead by the time they got him to the hospital. End of story.'

'No ideas?'

'No. One of the boys with Joey says he thought it was a dark Ford, but he could hardly see straight either. Anyway, I expect your boys have already got that.'

'That's right. No other ideas?'

Bowyer caught the tone of Sander's voice. 'Such as what?' he said quietly.

'Well, when something like the great

plague begins to hit Owen's boys and then one of your top men gets cut down in the prime of life, people could be excused for thinking there is some sort of hassle going on between you and Owen.'

'Then people would be wrong.'

'Possibly. Try and convince me.'

Bowyer scrubbed his chin with one hand and looked at Sander thoughtfully. 'We right off the record Mr Sander?'

'I don't see anyone else here.' Sander gave an exaggerated look round the office. 'Yes, we're off the record – unless you're going to confess to these couple of murders.'

'No way Mr Sander.' Bowyer grinned then rubbed his chin again. 'All right, it did look as though I might have a little bit of something brewing with Owen back at the beginning of the year. He started to sort of nibble round the edge of my, er, interests. Apparently someone was giving him a rough time and cutting down his movements a bit.' He gave Sander a suggestive look.

'Rough on him,' Sander murmured. 'Go on.'

'Well I took a look at what he was doing and decided that it wasn't worth getting into a sweat about it. It didn't amount to much and I figured it wouldn't last anyway.'

'Philanthropic, or just losing your bottle?'

'Neither.' Bowyer's face tightened a little. 'Just a businessman Mr Sander, and in business you don't start a lot of bother to cure something that will probably cure itself. And I was right. It cleared up as soon as Owen got his expenses, or whatever he was after.'

'And you let it die?'

'What else?' Bowyer gave Sander an assessing look before carrying on. 'And, still as a businessman and still very much off the record. If I had wanted to settle anything with Owen, I would have hired me an expert to go straight to the top and not mess round the edges like these nutters are doing. Without Owen that mob would be nothing.'

Sander nodded thoughtfully. Within the context of his own existence, Bowyer was making a lot of sense. 'And what about Owen? He might have picked up the wrong end of the stick and started to hit back – like with Waylett for instance to begin with.'

Bowyer shook his head slowly. 'I don't think so Mr Sander. Like I said, there's nothing to pick up and though Owen's a raver once he gets going.' He paused and tapped his temple. 'He's a cold man up here and doesn't blow until he's very sure.'

Again, Sander felt agreement, then went back over the conversation. 'You said – these nutters. More than one?'

'The way I figure it.' Bowyer paused for a moment's thought. 'I don't know anyone in this manor who runs to machine guns and bombs and most experts got there own special way. Yeah – I think more than one.'

There was something in Sander that disagreed this time and he gave Bowyer a long, level look while he thought about it. Bowyer faced it without blinking. Eventually, Sander nodded. 'All right, I believe you – but that still leaves you in a lot of bother.'

For a brief moment, Bowyer's eyes flickered, then veiled just as quickly as Sander wondered what nerve he had touched.

'In what way Mr Sander?' Bowyer said carefully.

'Well, my believing you doesn't make a lot of difference at the moment. I've got some superiors who believe otherwise and that means that you and all your doings will be in for a lot of attention from now on. As a businessman, I don't have to tell you how awkward that might be.'

Bowyer considered the statement carefully then looked deep into Sander's passive face. 'And there's a way out of that?'

'There's a way to cut it short. The sooner we pick up the killer or killers, the sooner you get back to normal. Now it occurs to me that a man with your connections might pick up a few items which normally wouldn't come our way and that it would be good business to pass them straight on to me as soon as you did. What do you think?'

Bowyer's face was also passive but his voice was hard. 'I think if the boot was on the other foot, we might be talking about blackmail Mr Sander.'

'That's a hard word,' Sander murmured absently. 'I prefer to think of it as co-operation.' His voice suddenly got as hard as Bowyer's. 'Well?'

There was a silence while Bowyer considered, then the humour that was in him peeped through and he grinned. 'All right Mr Sander, I'll, er, co-operate.' His grin got a little wider. 'Who'd have thought that I'd finish up as a grass – and for you.'

'It's a funny old world,' Sander said.

Bowyer nodded, then his grin took on a touch of craftiness. 'Mind you, as a businessman, I always think that one favour deserves another.'

'Do you?' Sander grunted as he heaved himself out of his chair. 'Well you carry on thinking that – and a lot of bloody good it will do you.'

Bowyer's face lost all its humour as he watched Sander's back moving towards the door.

10

Detective Chief Superintendent Unwin was not a happy man as he addressed the assembled investigation team gathered in the incident room. It was five weeks since Big Charlie Tooke had shuffled off his mortal coil and in those five weeks, Unwin had learned that publicity was very much a two-sided coin. A boon to the successful, it was quite the reverse for the unsuccessful, a fact which was more than galling to a man with Unwin's ambitions.

His frustration showed in his voice. He did not rant and rave, that was not Unwin's way. Rather, he was sorrowful. Sorrowful that he had been let down; sorrowful that the men he had picked had not lived up to the high hopes he had of them; sorrowful that the team leaders had not been able to impart to the team the urgency and drive which he himself would have given had he but the time to spare from his other pressing duties. Unwin was not only administering rebukes, he was preparing the ground for him to slide gently out from under him when blame came to be apportioned.

He named no names but, seated on a wooden, folding chair towards the front of the now-swollen team, Sander could feel the irritation building up with each squirm in Tripp, seated alongside him. That the irritation would be passed on to him later, he had no doubt, but he was strangely uncaring. It had been a long five weeks of boring leg-work, dead ends, information which led nowhere and clues which petered out almost as soon as they were obtained. He was tired.

Perhaps Unwin was right, he thought wryly. The drive had gone out of the team. A man could only gaze at a blank wall for so long. Perhaps... But no. He ought to be at least listening to the old man just in case he said something which did not contain a barely-hidden barb.

He switched his mind back to the room in time to hear Unwin intoning gravely and sincerely. 'I know – from long experience – how the lack of answers can build up into frustration...'

Five miles away, Sylvia Hawkins was experiencing that same frustration as she stood in the corridor outside her flat, both arms supporting over-filled shopping bags, while she jammed an elbow against the bell push to the infinite danger of the topmost shopping peeping out of the bags.

Damn you Den, come on, she thought irritably, as she went through the operation again. If she had to put these down one of them was bound to spill over – and her purse was halfway down the right-hand bag. Come on blast you.

She would not mind if he were busy, but there was not much hope of that. He would be sprawled in a chair watching that blasted telly without really seeing it and puffing smoke all over the place just the same as he had for nearly all of the past five weeks. Not lifting a finger to help, not talking – and not earning. And that was something else they needed to sort out soon. She had been used to money in plenty and it was getting a bit tight. Come on Den, for Christ sake.

She gave one, last, vicious jab at the bell-push then set the bags down with a mumbled curse. She had been right. One of them did spill over. She cursed again, sorted out her purse, took out her key and opened the flat door.

'Den,' she called. 'Come and give us a hand.'

She got no answer but the muted rumble of a television programme wafting down the little hall. Once again she swore, then dragged the shopping bags through the door and into the kitchen on the other side of the hall. She returned to slam the door viciously and start up the hall with battle in her greenish eyes and anger on her attractive, but hard, face.

'Den. Are you flaming well deaf?'

She hit the living room at a little rush then checked and surveyed the room. The television set flickered and chattered as she had expected but the low armchair conveniently in front of it was empty. Her eyes looked puzzled for a moment then moved on to the large envelope and piece of crumpled newspaper on the floor near it. They began to heat again. Now he was throwing rubbish all over the place. Did he think that she had nothing better to do than to pick up after him?

Again her gaze moved on, then suddenly rivetted as it met the sight of the lower legs and feet sticking out from beyond the back of the settee. One foot was still in a carpet slipper, the other, stockinged, seemed to be tense and twisted as though trying to imitate a clenched hand.

Shock froze her for a moment, then she muttered, 'Den?' and moved slowly across the room. She skirted the settee cautiously and gazed at the figure, face down behind it. 'Den?' she repeated hesitantly then got down on one knee beside the still body. For a long moment she stared disbelievingly at the two, small pieces of wooden dowel standing up from the back of the neck on thin wire, nodding grotesquely like some weird, child's toy then she stretched out a quivering hand to turn the head and gaze into the face of her ex-husband.

The hand recoiled sharply and as the breath hissed out of her, formed a knuckled fist to jam between her whitened lips. She was never sure afterwards that she was actually screaming or whether the shrieks were only inside her head.

It seemed to take a long time for the noise to stop, the teeth-indented knuckles to come out, and for her to rise and stumble across the room to the telephone

'Just a little more effort. That extra bit when it hardly seems worthwhile. That, it seems to me is what is needed. I think...'

Chief Superintendent Unwin's voice was larded with sincerity but he had lost

Inspector Sander again.

His attention was occupied by the young, W.P.C. who had just entered the room through the door at the side of the incident room. She had a message flimsy in her hand and a very worried expression on her face. Her problem was obvious, the message was important and she had been told to deliver it right away – but how did one interrupt a Godly figure like Unwin when in full flight?

He nudged Tripp in the ribs, got an indignant grunt in reply, then jerked his head in the direction of the waiting girl.

Tripp followed his jerk, frowned at the girl for a moment then motioned her over. She scuttled across the room on semi-tip-toe and leaned over Tripp. Unwin, who had not missed a single motion, frowned loftily but carried on smoothly.

'It's supposed to be for the D.C.S., sir,' the girl whispered as Tripp extended his hand for the message.

'He'll get it,' Tripp grunted as he took it from her with an abrupt motion.

The watching Sander saw the consternation dawn on his face as he read the message then heard the explosive: 'Jesus Christ,' burst from his lips.

Tripp dropped the flimsy into Sander's lap

then stood up abruptly and made for Unwin. He let it lay there, still watching Tripp, then saw the muttered discussion and the same baffled amazement spread over Unwin's face. Only then did he pick up the message and skim through it.

There was not a lot there. Merely a laconic report that one, Dennis Hawkins, had been found dead in his flat, strangled by... A what? A cheese cutter?

11

It was a smaller meeting this time and the four, big men jammed round the desk seemed to fill all the available space in the office Tripp had been using.

Unwin, his smooth face and diplomatic manner put aside for once, showing some of the iron which had also been needed to carry him so far up his chosen ladder; Tripp, emitting brooding frustration; Gander, unaffected by the aura of either man, twiddling an innocuous-looking length of wire attached to two, wooden handles between his fat hands; and Sander, a little withdrawn, feeling rather like the poor boy from next door who has been asked to the party purely from courtesy.

'Do you have to fiddle with that thing?' Unwin asked sharply as Gander twitched the wire yet again.

'Sorry,' Gander said equably but kept the instrument in his hands.

Tripp also looked at it then shook his big head. 'A bloody cheese cutter. This thing's getting crazier and crazier.'

'Strictly speaking, no,' Gander told him. 'I suppose that name fits it but for my money, it was made up specially to suit the man who was going to use it.' He stretched the wire between his immense arms. 'Look how short it is for me.'

'Not another expert,' Sander murmured.

'Very much so Jack, I should say. Very, very much so.'

There was a silence while Gander gazed at the wire, then Tripp rumbled: 'All right then, you've got us all on edge, so let's have it.'

Gander twinkled at him benignly. 'You are getting touchy these days Dave.'

'The expert – remember?' Tripp reminded him heavily.

'Ah yes. Well now, there are a number of things which point that way. As I've said. I think this thing was tailor-made. Then there's the attack itself. Most stranglers are pretty violent affairs with lots of signs of a hard struggle. What did we have here? Just a bit of scuffed carpet and that was all. Why? Because this lad knew exactly how and where to hit.'

'There's a correct spot?' Sander asked with a frown.

'There certainly is Jack but, oddly enough, the vast majority of amateurs never hit it. For some reason they invariably go for the base of the throat when in actual fact on or above the thyroid cartilage is far more effective.'

'The what?' Tripp queried shortly.

'The Adam's apple to you Dave.'

'Hmp,' Tripp grunted.

'And this boy hit that?' Sander said.

'Right on the button. So much so that it was fractured. And that brings us to another point. In this country, where mechanical strangulation isn't the art that it is in some others, most killers drop the rope or scarf or stocking or whatever it happens to be, over the victim's head and then pull across their chest with crossed hands. Like this.' Gander crossed his arms over his big chest. 'See how much effort you have to put into it to get real power. Now in the east and places like that, they drop a loop over the victim's head and then all the power can go in one hard, outward thrust. See.' He placed his hands together on his chest and threw them outward with an explosive force that made the wire twang. 'And that's it – bang. The initial impact does so much that there's not a lot of resistance in the latter stages. Yes friends, a real expert.'

Sander grimaced at the thought and there was a little silence while the others seemed similarly affected.

'Charming,' Unwin said eventually. 'Anything else?'

'Not really Super. Attacked from behind, of course. Apart from the position of the instrument, there were contusions on the nose and chin when the killer let the victim fall.'

'And that's important,' Tripp put in. 'It means that Hawkins knew the killer.'

'Why?' Unwin asked shortly.

Tripp looked a little put out and it reflected in his voice. 'Well, it stands to reason sir. After what happened to Tooke and Adkin, Owen and what's left of his crew would suss anyone who came knocking at their doors and they wouldn't be letting them in unless they knew and trusted them.'

'I don't know that we can place too much reliance on that,' Unwin said thoughtfully. 'Look at the number of people who do have legal access and look at the number of times we are called in when it is faked. The man with a book and pencil in his hand who has come to read the meter and finishes up banging some old lady over the head. The man with some sort of gauge looking for a gas leak who clears everyone out of the house on safety grounds and then cleans the place out. Even the boy with a fake warrant card. We've seen enough of them Dave – and it was five weeks ago since the Tooke affair. A man doesn't stay on his guard for ever.'

Sander felt a measure of agreement and looked at Unwin thoughtfully.

'I know all that,' Tripp argued. 'But I still can't see Hawkins letting a stranger in and taking his eyes off of him long enough to give him a clean run at his back.'

'I thought of that,' Unwin told him and tapped the envelope and smoothed-out piece of newspaper on the desk in front of him. 'And I think that is where this comes into it. You've read it, of course?'

'Of course,' Tripp rapped.

'And you Jack?' Unwin turned his gaze onto Sander.

Sander smelt a trap but said: 'Yes sir.'

'And it doesn't give you any ideas?'

Sander thought hard then shook his head. 'Not really sir. It's just a front page splash about a big, drug haul and how the port boys cracked it. It was a damned good bit of work but I don't really see what it had to do with this.'

'That's precisely the point Jack. Precisely the point.' Unwin paused a moment to savour his triumph before carrying on: 'Now let us suppose that you are a villain like Hawkins and someone – even a perfect stranger – hands you an envelope and asks you to read its contents. It won't take you long to find out that it concerns a crime which is nothing to do with you, but, being a criminal, you are going to carry right on to the end to make damned sure of that fact. The only latent prints we lifted from that envelope and paper belonged to Hawkins but I'll bet a good bit of my pension that he never got to finish reading it.'

Sander pictured the scene and nodded slowly. It made damned good sense and once again he looked at Unwin thoughtfully. So the man wasn't just a diplomatic face, he thought. But then he had to be more, didn't he? A man did not get to be D.C.S. in this man's police force on oil alone. 'Could very well be sir.'

'It sounds right,' Tripp admitted grudgingly. 'This is a real clever mob.'

'Mob?' Sander queried quietly.

'Mob.' Tripp repeated heavily. 'And like I say, clever. They know that one man committing all the killings in one way would narrow the field right down. This way they spread it out into a big likely field.'

'I agree,' Unwin said and Gander nodded. Sander neither spoke nor moved. He still kept coming back to the simple, grim solution of a practical criminal like Bowyer. One expert to take the top man out and the rest would fold. It was cheap and effective and suited the criminal minds that he had always encountered. This other business was too bizarre to fit into ordinary patterns of behaviour.

The lack of action was noted by Unwin. 'You don't agree Inspector?'

'I'm sorry sir, I don't.' Sander took a breath and looked directly into Tripp's narrowed eyes. 'It's as I argued with the Chief Inspector, if someone had wanted to widen the field, they would have picked run of the mill killers. An ordinary gunman, a straight bomber who works with jelly wired to the ignition switch and that sort of thing. And now this weirdy – a professional strangler. They're not widening the field, they are narrowing it to a bunch of head cases.'

'Are you suggesting that we are then looking for one super-killer with all the talents?' Unwin asked with more than a touch of mockery.

Narrowed down to that, it did sound lame and Sander shrugged uncomfortably under Unwin's supercilious stare and Tripp's hard look. 'I don't know sir,' he admitted, then added stubbornly. 'But I think it makes as much sense as the other theory.'

There was a strained silence, finally broken by Gander.

'Yes Jack, perhaps. But this way could be very clever as well. If they aimed for confusion, you've got to admit that they have succeeded – we're damned confused.'

'That I disagree with,' Unwin cut in sharply. 'There's no confusion in my mind. We are after a well-directed gang of assassins. Who is directing them and why, we have yet to fathom out but we'll get to him when we get one or more of them. And that is the priority, Dave. Deeper digging, wider digging. Plus of course, a lot tighter surveillance on the two remaining potential targets.' He paused fractionally and directed a sharp look at Tripp. 'There should have been a bit more on Hawkins.'

'We had a car there,' Tripp said wearily. 'But there are sixty flats in that building and five ways of getting in and out. They could only cover the main entrance for known or suspicious characters and follow Hawkins when he went out. To seal the place up, we would have needed half the force.'

'Hmm,' Unwin grunted, managing to convey a seed of doubt even though he knew Tripp to be right. 'Anyway, our area has narrowed now and we should be able to do better – we have to do better. With a little extra vigilance and a little more drive, I am convinced...'

His voice began to drone out the same platitudes he had uttered on the previous day and Sander felt his mind slipping away from them. He had heard it all before. His eyes wandered to the killing wire in Gander's hands then on to the sheet of newspaper on the desk then – he halted at the flip-over calendar beside the paper. October the thirty-first. No, that was wrong. That had been the day of the killing – yesterday. Today was November. Someone had not turned the calendar. Very remiss in a room they had known that the exalted Detective Chief Superintendent was going to use. He would have to point that out to Inspector Berry and watch the expression on his face. Yes, today was November all right. Thirty days hath... His mind began on the old jingle, then checked. October – September – August. It fitted. The mind began to move on to new ground.

It figured on to the background of Unwin's voice until he broke it by standing abruptly. 'Right then Dave, that's the procedure.' He looked at Gander. 'Are you coming back with me?'

Gander nodded and lumbered to his feet. Sander also rose, half automatically, nodded to their farewells and then sat down again as Tripp escorted them to the door. He was deep in thought again by the time Tripp closed the door and turned to look at him.

He looked at him for a long moment, his face slightly puzzled, then said gruffly: 'What's this – more sulks?'

'Eh?' Sander came out of his deep thought to look back at Tripp.

'Are you sulking again because you are the only one with your ideas?' Tripp amplified.

'No Dave,' Sander said slowly. 'I think I might have got some sort of pattern out of this nutty business.'

Tripp came back and sat on the opposite side of the desk. 'Well?'

Sander groped for words to outline the ideas which were still forming. 'It's not really all falling in yet – but it's all to do with Owen.'

'Surprise – surprise,' Tripp said with ponderous irony.

'No, wait Dave. I don't mean just on the criminal side – this gang warfare thing – but on the personal side.'

Tripp frowned. 'Personal? In what way?'

'Well start with the times of the jobs. One in August, one in September, and this last one in October. One a month, building up, and Owen beginning to sweat more each time.'

'Mm. Bit thin.'

'But is it? Let's look at the killings. Witnesses peering through that factory door have placed everyone for us. Tall thin man by the box, big man clubbing the guard, little man in between – and another man blasting away with a shotgun at the hedge. With Dew at the wheel, that's got to be Owen.'

'So?'

'So why didn't this joker pick him off then? He's a crack shot, according to Goosey, and he's got a man with his head and shoulders over the top of a van door firing at him. Wouldn't you take him out first?'

'Maybe. Maybe this lad wanted to stop Tooty getting that box.'

'If he had blown the top of Owen's head off instead, that would have stopped them just as well. And look at afterwards. Some wide shots through the van door and a few high up through the side where he knew he would hit nobody. No, that boy wanted only one on that trip – and anyone but Owen.'

'It's feasible I suppose,' Tripp conceded slowly.

'More than feasible when you look at the other two. Take Big Charlie's car. Why wait a month to booby-trap that when Owen's had been sitting in the same yard for all of that month presenting an easier target most of the time? Because a month was the allotted time and it was still not Owen's turn. And it was the same yesterday. If he could have walked in on Hawkins and got in a position to throttle him, then he could have done it just as easy to Owen. I tell you Dave, it's all calculated for maximum effect and friend Owen is last on the list.'

'Mm.' Tripp was silently thoughtful as he studied Sander. Relations between the two men had been stiffly formal since they had clashed weeks ago. Both were proud, stubborn men, neither given to admitting that there might have been faults on either side. But Tripp was too good a thief-taker to allow that to influence his judgement even though the theory edged against some of his own pre-conceived notions of the case. 'Yes – it makes sense,' he conceded finally. 'But it doesn't really split the thing wide open, does it? If you're right, we've got a little edge. They'll hit Dew next and we can concentrate on him.'

'Unless...' Sander said slowly. The idea that had started with his recognition of the time factor was building on within him, taking a more concrete shape.

'Unless what?' Tripp demanded, eyes suddenly narrowed.

'Unless we force a little bit more of an edge from it. Look Dave, we can guard Dew all we want but you know what it's like trying to protect a man twenty-four hours a day over a long period. The other side can pick their time and perfect their plan while we just stand around wondering when the crunch is going to come. We're damned vulnerable even under the best circumstances.'

'All right, I know it, but that's the way the game's played.'

'Well suppose we play it a little different.' Sander paused a moment to straighten his mind. 'Suppose we put them on the wrong foot – force them into a few hurried changes? Suppose we put everything we can spare round Dew, openly and not too cleverly –

even woollies in their reach-me-down rain-coats with their uniforms and ties peeping out of the tops?'

Tripp shrugged a little impatiently. 'They'd do a quick change of plan and go after Owen, I suppose.'

'Damned right. And we both know that a quick change of plan could give us that edge we are on about.'

Tripp went into thought again, then nodded slowly. 'You could be right. These things are nervy at the best of times, even with pros. Yes, they could get careless. But what happens to your friend Owen?'

'We'll put some real undercover men around him. This lot must expect him to recruit a bit of protection and some of those long-haired cowboys you've got at Regional look more like villains than villains do. We could have one with him at all times wired up to a car full of picked men tucked away out of sight but not reach.'

'And that's supposed to stop them getting at him?'

'It's a good chance. They'll be off balance a bit to start with and they'll be expecting to deal with muscle-bound yobs and not trained men in instant communication with others.'

Again Tripp nodded. 'Could work,' he conceded then looked directly at Sander. 'And it could go badly wrong.'

Sander shrugged. 'Anything can go wrong – but it's still better than waiting around with masses of men, knowing that, if they care to wait, we're going to have to pull off sooner or later and leave the targets open anyway.'

'True – but if it does blow up, your tethered goat is going to get the chopper.'

Sander's face set. 'Owen's where he is because of what he is. He chose the path. I don't see that we have to get in a muck sweat about his hide.'

A hard grin pulled at Tripp's lips and he shook his head. 'You know Jack, every now and again the word goes round that you've got a bit soft.' He paused and his grin widened. 'It's a bloody lie.'

Sander flushed a little at the barbed truth in the statement. 'We're after a mass killer – or killers,' he defended lamely.

'Who, if we're cold-blooded and practical about it, will get Owen anyway if we don't get them first,' Tripp finished for him. 'Quite true but, according to the book, Owen is just another law-abiding citizen who we are supposed to protect at all times.'

'The difference between what the book

says and actually taking villains is a damned long mile,' Sander grunted.

'I hope you're not thinking of quoting that to the press in the near future?' Tripp said, getting his grin back. Then the grin faded. 'Still, it's not a bad notion of yours. At least it gives us something concrete to do instead of wading through all this damned paper and waiting for them to hit us where and when they choose in the meantime.' He paused then looked at Sander searchingly. 'Why didn't you come out with this when the D.C.S. was here?'

'I didn't get the idea about the time sequence until the meeting was all but over and the rest came when he was half-way out of the door. In any case.' He returned Tripp's look. 'He hasn't exactly got the reputation of being a bit of a gambler.'

'And I have?'

'You've been known to cut a few corners in the past.'

Tripp's hard look took on a musing quality. 'Yeah – the past,' he said quietly, thought for a moment, then added suddenly. 'How long have you got to go Jack?'

Sander frowned at the abrupt change of subject and said: 'Too long – it seems sometimes.'

'I've got about eighteen months.' Tripp's voice was still musing.

Sander nodded while his mind groped for the connection but before he could grasp it, Tripp changed tack again.

'Know much about Unwin?'

Again Sander groped. 'Not a lot. Gossip mainly. He's supposed to be smart – and political.'

Tripp nodded. 'Both true. And, as you say, he doesn't take chances.' Tripp checked, put the tips of his fingers together and looked at Sander over the top of them. 'And, under all that smooth veneer, he's damned hard and carries the can for no one.'

Sander slowly put the apparently disjointed conversation together. 'Which means...' he began.

'Which means that the past is the past and that I don't fancy spending those last eighteen months looking after the traffic boys on the motorway,' Tripp supplied for him.

'So the idea is out?' Sander tried to control the chagrin in his tone.

'Tempting as it is, as far as I am concerned, yes,' Tripp said quietly then lowered his eyes to stare at the desk in a silence which lasted long enough to bring the puzzled frown back to Sander's face. When he looked up again, his expression was absolutely wooden. 'In fact, apart from your theory about timing, I don't recall hearing any idea.'

Quick questions flooded into Sander's mind then he looked into Tripp's wooden face, saw something lurking behind his eyes and stayed silent.

Tripp seemed to give the faintest nod of approval then stirred the papers on the desk. 'Now, to business. You're going to need all the men you can get and I've got three bright D.C.s down at Regional who look less like coppers than anything you ever saw that you might be able to use.'

'*I* might be able to use?'

'Yes, you. You heard the D.C.S., he wants top surveillance on the remaining two. With this local knowledge we keep hearing about and your close connections with Berry and his uniformed mob, I think you're the logical man to take over the job. It's yours.' Tripp's face seemed to get even more expressionless. 'With full responsibility.'

The words hammered home and Sander's face suddenly matched Tripp's as his mind flooded with a swirl of thoughts. There was resentment at first. Resentment coupled with disappointment in a man he had long respected. They burned for a quick moment and then fairness tinged with a little compassion crept in. Would he be so eager to toss away a long career, now nearing its close, on a gambler's chance when there was little to be gained personally from that chance? But then wasn't that the choice that he was being given to a lesser degree? And for what? To give Mr bloody Chief Superintendent Unwin another boost up the ladder? Or to protect Owen and the likes of Owen? Owen. It always came back to Owen. This lot were killers but behind all the effort he had put in to catching them was the thought that they must know something which would put him away with them. He hated to admit it to his policeman's mind, but that had been his biggest motivation all along. So was it still a motivation and had he the conviction to make the decisions he had expected others to make for him?

'Full responsibility sir?' he queried quietly.

A faint sadness seemed to invade Tripp's wooden face for a moment, then he nodded shortly. 'That's right. You're a senior, responsible officer with a good record. You don't need me peering over your shoulder on a job like that every five minutes, do you?'

Sander paused for just a second. Owen – Owen – Owen. 'No sir,' he said firmly. 'I can manage it quite well on my own.'

12

Apart from Tom Munson, there were three men in Owen's waiting room. One lounged behind the counter close to Munson, the other two sat and read newspapers without paying too much attention to them. They had similar hard eyes, careful faces and easy-moving bodies. The two holding papers put them down and came to their feet lightly as Sander moved up the room with Blackman in tow and made to skirt the counter. He got as far as the suddenly-outstretched arm of the third man.

'Going somewhere chum?' the man asked quietly.

Sander checked and looked him up and down slowly then turned to glance at the other two who had closed silently in behind them. Owen had moved quickly, and he had bought well by the look of them. They looked tough and competent. London, he guessed by the clothes and the accent. A little lightness lifted the near-depression which had been on him since his interview with Tripp. It was starting. In for a penny, in for a pound.

'Just popping in to see Owen,' he said with deceptive mildness.

The man let his eyes slide away from him to Blackman's bulk. 'He expecting you?'

'I doubt it.'

The restraining arm turned into a big, heavily-ringed hand flat against his chest. 'On your bike then chum.'

Sander looked at the hand and then at the face behind it. 'Who are you?'

The man gave a short, barking laugh. 'What's that to you chum?'

'Oh, I like to know in advance who I am nicking,' Sander said casually.

The hand dropped away smartly and the man took a quick step backwards. 'Law?'

'Right first time sonny.' Sander took out his warrant card and dangled it under the man's nose. 'Read it and weep.'

The man flicked a quick glance over it then recovered and gave a tight grin. 'Ok, so maybe you do get to see Owen after all.'

'First things first,' Sander said mildly then his voice tightened as he stabbed a finger at each man in turn. 'You, you and you. You'll be on your way back to the Smoke within an hour or I'll run you in so fast your feet won't touch.'

The man blinked then got his grin back. 'You country coppers like to throw your weight around, don't you?'

'Don't read it wrong lad,' Sander warned grimly. 'We're near enough to London to have picked up a lot of your bad habits. This is a tough, little town and we're well used to dealing with tough, little lads. So what's it going to be – are you on your way, or inside?'

'For what?' the man asked, his hard eyes beginning to heat.

'Well, let's see.' Sander looked at the trio and made a shrewd guess. 'I should think carrying concealed weapons might do for a start.' Two of the men stiffened and he grinned smugly. 'Then there's obstructing an officer in the course of, and all that. Assault. Resisting arrest.'

'What arrest?' the man broke in.

Sander leaned forward slightly. 'The one that is going to take place any damned minute now sonny.'

There was a short silence. The face of the man in front of Sander began to set mulishly then one of the men behind said suddenly: 'Come on Terry, swallow it. There's nothing but rasher for us here.'

The silence came again, then the man

shrugged and began to skirt Sander and Blackman. 'You're all the bloody same, you lot,' he muttered bitterly as he did so.

'True sonny, true,' Sander beamed at him. 'Now – what was it? Oh yeah – on your bike.'

Sander went through the door to Owen's office in his usual fashion. Half turned away, standing behind the desk, Owen got out a smothered exclamation, pivotted and lunged pantherishly towards the right-hand side of the desk. Then his mind registered Sander and Blackman and he checked and froze.

'Why the hell don't you learn to knock?' he rasped with a thin edge of panic in his tone.

'Sorry. No upbringing,' Sander said equably and looked at him searchingly. He was a different Owen. A lot of the superficial veneer had peeled away revealing the hard, dangerous animal beneath. He was rattled, but he had not cracked. With his mentality, he probably never would, Sander thought.

His eyes went past Sander and Blackman to the empty corridor behind them and he frowned. 'How the hell did you march straight in here anyway?'

Sander grinned faintly. 'Past your hard-case reception committee, you mean? Oh I sent them away.'

'You did what?'

'I told them I'd nick them if I saw them hanging round here again. It was quite simple.'

There was a moment while Owen visibly mastered his quick anger, then he said in a hard, flat voice: 'What sort of a game are you playing Sander?'

'Mr Sander, to you,' Sander reminded him quietly. 'And the game is called, law and order. We've got enough trouble at the moment without you importing hair-trigger muscle which is likely to explode all over the place at the slightest provocation. Not in my patch you don't Owen.'

Owen got out a short, scornful laugh. 'Law and order is it? The sort of law and order that stops a man protecting himself.' He nodded slowly and gave Sander a keen look. 'Yeah, I think I see the sort of law and order you've got in mind – Sander.'

'You'll get protection,' Sander said quickly. 'But the right sort of protection – from us.'

'You – protecting me? Yeah, I can imagine the sort of effort you'll put into that. No thank you. I'll get my own and if you try to push them around we'll see what my brief's got to say about harassment and all that sort of thing. You might not look too good at the end of that Sander. That's law and order.'

Sander's face set. 'You can forget it. The time's over for that, model citizen, fanny. For some reason, someone is out to do for the whole bunch of you. Now the thought of that doesn't exactly leave me prostrate, but then I'm not an advocate of murder either so you'll get your protection – even if I have to ram it down your neck.'

His tone got through to Owen and he looked at him thoughtfully. 'What sort of protection then?'

'You'll have a man with you at all times and there'll be another car load only seconds away.' Sander tried to put conviction into his voice but it did nothing to enlarge the sparseness of the cover he was proposing.

'One man – one car?'

'A tough, well-trained man. A specialist. He'll be a lot more use to you than any of those goons you had out there.'

'In a pig's eye. Bloody hell, that's inviting...'

Owen checked suddenly, put his knuckles on the table between them and leaned forward to stare into Sander's face with

171

narrowed eyes. 'That's it. You're setting me up you bastard. Bare enough cover to pull these nutters towards me and perhaps just enough to give you a chance to collar them.' He gave another short laugh. 'And all this righteous chat about law and order. You cold-blooded bastard.'

'Rubbish,' Sander growled, holding his own eyes firm to meet Owen's accusing gaze but knowing that, yet again, he had under-estimated the razor-sharpness of the man's mind. 'And watch your lip.'

'Balls. You said yourself that all that fanny was over. Ok, it is, but if you think that's going to make me lie down as bait for you, then you're out of your flatfooted mind. I'm getting my own protection Sander and if you get round that with your law and order twaddle, then I'll take it on my toes.'

'Where will you go? The Smoke – Brum? You'll stand a lot of chance there won't you? No money, no connections, and out in the open.'

'I got by there before on my own and I'll do it again. Don't worry about me copper, you just worry about finding yourself another goat.'

Sander's eyes still held Owen's, firm and steady, but behind them he was feeling the building of the old, familiar frustration which always seemed to come when he tried to bend this man to his will. He should have known the moment he burst through that door and saw that he was still the tough... His thoughts veered back. When he burst through the door, Owen was...

He walked slowly round the desk.

Owen watched him, wary and puzzled, started to back away, then checked, his eyes filled with sudden alarm as Sander reached for the top drawer of the desk. The drawer he had started to dive for. 'Hey – you got no right...'

Sander ignored him and slid open the drawer. A slow grin crossed his face as he gazed down at the Browning automatic nestling on top of the papers there. 'Well, well. What have we here?' He took out a handkerchief and used it to pick out the gun carefully, two fingers on either side of the trigger guard, and dangled it before Owen's suddenly-fixed face. 'You've got a licence for this, of course?'

'Save the corny jokes for the policemen's concert,' Owen said defiantly.

Sander carried on grinning. 'Oh let me enjoy myself just a little bit – I've waited long enough.' He transferred his grin to

Blackman. 'Let's see Sergeant, fourteen years for possession with intent to injure at the moment, isn't it?'

Blackman's grin was as wide as his. 'Something like that governor.'

'What bloody intent to injure?' Owen demanded heatedly.

'Oh, I expect we can think of something between us, given a little time. It did seem to me that you might have had that drawer open and your hand on it when we came through the door. What do you think Sergeant?'

'It's a moot point all right,' Blackman agreed gravely.

'You and your law and order,' Owen said bitterly.

Sander felt a quick stab of something inside, but pushed it down. 'Yeah. And you leaned on it so long that it broke.' He put the gun onto a clean sheet of paper on the desk and looked at Owen quizzically. 'Now, about this protection we are going to give you.'

'Are we really staking him out?' Blackman asked as he started the engine.

The words cut across Sander's jumbled thoughts as he put the carefully-wrapped gun into the glove-box. There was the irony that at last he had something concrete on Owen and could not use it for now; the further irony that he was taking a chance with his own career to protect Owen and yet perhaps risking his life in the process; and, above all these, the disquieting knowledge that, with this case and his obsession with Owen, he was being slowly driven further down the road he had so often condemned others for taking. The end-justifies-the-means road where the maintenance of law merged into a uniform greyness with the evil it was trying to eliminate.

'Don't you start talking bloody rubbish as well,' he snapped.

Blackman dipped the clutch and meshed the gears angrily. He admired the Old Man, even liked him as a person, but there were some days when you just couldn't put a damned foot right with him.

13

Detective Constable Reg Caller was young, tough, smart and thought a lot of himself. He had good reason for the last. He had graduated well, spent the minimum time in uniform, and, since being made detective, had built up an enviable reputation as one of the young ones who would go places. True, his informal dress and manner and approach raised a few conservative eyebrows but he considered them an asset in the career he had already mapped out for himself.

He put down the magazine he had been loafing through, crossed one leg over the other and looked thoughtfully across the office to where Owen's head was bent over his desk. And this job could do him a bit of good as well, if it broke right and he was lucky enough to be around when it did. Of course, that might not be for a few weeks yet, according to that old bird Sander who had warned him and Batson and Temple to be more on their guard as the month lengthened but that was police work all over and he had the sort of mentality that could conjure up unlimited patience when there was the possibility of a profitable end result.

Queer old cuss, that Sander. Not really the sort of bod you would expect to be running a tight set up like this. More of a go-by-the-book man. Had a good rep though, in a plodding sort of way. But then something must have kept him tied to a backwater like...

There was a light tap at the door.

Caller settled the regulation issue .38 in its holster and nodded to Owen's enquiring look.

'Come in,' Owen called.

The door opened and Tom Munson slid in with his usual diffident manner. 'Sorry to bother you Mr Owen, but there's a phone call.' He nodded towards Caller. 'For Mr Caller.'

'Well put the damned thing through here.' Owen's voice was edgy as he jerked his head at the telephone on his desk.

'Can't Mr Owen. The extension line don't work.'

Owen and Caller exchanged quick glances.

'Did he say who he was?' Caller asked.

Munson turned a puzzled face to him. 'Yes – funny – he said he was Inspector Sander.'

Caller stiffened. In this place only Owen was supposed to know that he was not what he seemed, a tough, young bodyguard. If Sander was breaking the cover, something must have gone up with a bang. 'Definitely, Inspector Sander?'

'That's what he said Mr Caller.'

Caller stood up and crossed to the door. Munson began to move out in front of him. Then the policeman in Caller checked and took quick, mental stock. The office was here, the corridor was there and the phone was at the end of the corridor in the outer office. With the door to that open and this open, he could damned near watch Owen all the time. His innate caution died. 'Keep this door open,' he told Owen as he left the room.

He was half-way down the passage when the light from the office began to fade and he realised how dim everything was. 'What the hell's wrong with the light,' he called to the indistinct back of Munson shambling along in the gloom before him.

'I don't know Mr Caller. It's not the bulb. I'd just checked that when that phone rang.

178

I'd better have a look at the fuse box.'
Munson's dim shape turned into one of the
openings leading off of the passage.

Caller muttered and carried on until he
reached the door leading to the outer office
then he jammed it open and took a quick
look back along the passage to the light
shining from Owen's door. Satisfied, he
turned his back and crossed the few feet to
the receiver lying on the counter.

'Hello sir,' he said.

A quiet, dead buzz answered him.

Instant suspicion took over but he could
not resist the natural impulse to repeat:
'Hello sir – hello – hello.' He swore and
began to replace the receiver. It was an
action he never completed.

He was never quite sure afterwards
whether he did hear a light tread behind
him or whether he did hear something sigh
softly through the air. He was only sure of
the pain behind his ear and the sudden
tunnel of blackness he lurched into.

There was a similar experience coming out
of the tunnel. There may have been a flicker
of movement from a figure just out of his
line of vision and he may have heard the
door to the passage close but both were so

uncertain that they flitted into his mind to be lost forever. His first real memory was finding himself on his knees and hands, his head hanging like a sick dog.

He groaned, shook his head, then lifted it to gaze at the closed door. Everything came back with a sudden rush that redoubled the pain in his head. Instinct took the place of training and he lurched to his feet and stumbled through the door. The darkened passage stretched out in front of him with, grimly, no light at the end. He sobbed and began to weave an erratic way up the passage then something tangled his feet and he went to his knees with a grunt of pain. For a moment, the pain drove everything away, then he swivelled on his knees, stretched out his hands in the near darkness and bent closer to the huddled thing which had tripped him.

It was a man. And there was blood, warm and sticky to his touch. Christ, there was blood everywhere. He bent even closer, trying to make the most of the light that filtered up from the office doorway. Too small for Owen. It had to be the other one. The old man. What the hell was his name? The action of forcing his brain to think of it reasserted his training and his fingers traced on until they located a weak pulse in the thin neck. Still alive. Shouldn't be moved. But then he was bleeding to death by the feel of it. He paused just for a moment to turn his head and gaze along at Owen's closed door but his instinct told him that there was nothing there for him except a severe check to his ambitions and what duty he had now was to the still living.

He weaved to his feet and began to drag the still form back to the outer office, leaving a long, sickening trail behind him.

In the office, he left the limp body on the floor and forced himself stubbornly towards the telephone. God, he felt worse than when he had first come to. He dialled with a shaking finger, gabbled a brief message then turned back to the form on the floor. For a moment, he peered at it helplessly. Where did you start with that much blood? Then his glazed, already-shadowed eyes located the main source pumping through the thin shirt covering the forearm.

He pulled off his belt and was still trying to fashion a clumsy tourniquet with awkward fingers when tyres screeched to a frantic halt outside the building.

Sander blinked against the glare of the

popping flashlights and surveyed the now crowded room. The photographers, the fingerprint boys, the measurers, the drawers of chalk lines. They all left him strangely unmoved. Almost as unmoved as the main actor in the scene. He was jammed back, upright, in his chair, fixed hands seemingly trying to crush the ends of the arms, wide eyes which held a shiny, dangerous glitter, even in death. All very typical. Sander did not need Gander on this one. Death from a knife was something he was a bit more familiar with. A chest thrust, the head thrown back and the mouth wide open where it had fought for a last despairing breath. All the normal signs of such a thrust. Delivered from behind, over the shoulder, Sander thought, looking at the height of the chair back and the room between the body and the desk. And done well. No signs of anything except one, hard, deliberately driven stroke.

The bloody expert again.

Even the right tool for the job. His eyes went down to the knife resting on a sheet of plastic on the desk. Eight-inch, tapering blade, twin, sharpened edges, and heavy enough to do half the work for the user if held steady and driven true. A military tool of some sort. The sort of thing that is issued, played with, instructed upon, and hardly ever used except to open a tin with. Except in this case.

And Owen had known the man and sat still for it. Or had he? Sander's eyes went over it again. That was a swivel chair with a high back. It could have been turned another way when the killer crept through the door which Caller had said he had instructed to be left open. Sander sighed lightly. Everything that ever happened in these cases seemed to conspire against him coming to one definite conclusion.

He sighed to himself again. Perhaps it was just as well that he was off it? Or would be shortly when initial impact of the crime was over and the wheels started turning. His eyes went back to Owen's body. He had helped to kill that man. Sure, all sorts of things could be argued. He had done what he thought to be best in difficult circumstances; even, morally, that Owen was a man who had deserved killing. But that did not stop it jarring violently against a lifetime's work and training. And would he have taken a chance like that with anyone else but Owen? An ordinary citizen – or even another criminal? It was a question he did not want to answer and the knowledge of that refusal left him jaded and drained. He felt vaguely like a man who had come to the end of a long quest only to find that there was nothing there.

It took effort to pull his mind away from his dark thoughts and turn to where Tripp was just straightening from hearing the seated Caller's story repeated yet again. Caller, with the slurred voice and black-ringed eyes of delayed concussion.

'All right lad. Now we had better get you some hospital attention.'

'I don't feel too bad,' Caller lied, attempting to salvage something. 'I can hang on if you can use me.'

Tripp shook his head. 'Not necessary. We're knee deep in help.' He nodded to an attendant constable. 'See that he gets there all right.' He watched Caller being helped out then turned to Sander and blew out his breath. 'I don't know, you train them and train them and then something happens and it goes out of the window. All that thrashing about in the dark and he could have called for help at any time on his radio.'

'No.' Sander shook his head. 'Oh he didn't think of it. Too confused. But it wouldn't have done him any good. We found his radio and his gun half-way up the passage.'

'Hmm. These boys think of everything, don't they. The gun and all eh? Not taking a chance on flogging it for a bit of extra profit.'

'Too traceable. Like you say, they think of everything.'

'No prints?'

'They're working on them now – but there'll be nothing.' Sander nodded across the room to the pair of blood-stained, rough, industrial gloves that lay beside the knife on the plastic sheet. 'We found those as well. They were just inside the passage door. I should think the gloves were the last thing to come off – and they're too rough to leave latents, even inside.'

'Odd, leaving the weapon like that,' Tripp frowned.

'Why not? Forensic would have told us what sort of knife we were looking for. Why cart it around with you?'

Tripp nodded. 'Yes, I suppose so. Christ, they're a cool lot.' He looked round the room. 'Anything else?'

'Only enough to bear out Caller's story. There was a forced entry through a window at the end of one of those side passages. A fuse block had been removed completely from the box – we found it dropped behind a radiator – and the phone extension-line had been chopped in the passage.'

Tripp thought it over slowly. 'So they break in, cut the wire, fix the lights and make the phone call. Then they stay in one of those passages until Caller's passed, thump him while he's bawling down an empty phone and then come and deal with Owen. Then what?'

Sander shrugged. 'Guesswork, but I should think they bumped into Munson as he came back from looking at the fuse box and they came out of Owen's. They knifed him to get him out of the way and then just walked out.'

'Leaving him alive,' Tripp added thoughtfully.

'Yes.' Sander sighed. 'And that's why I don't think he'll be any good to us. If he knew anything worth knowing, they would have finished him.'

'This lot – too damned right. How is the old man?'

'We're waiting to hear from the hospital now.'

'Well let's hope. But you're probably right, with our luck it'll turn into another damned dead end.' Tripp was silent for a moment, then said: 'Anyway, it proves that they are a mob.'

'It does?' Sander queried quietly.

'Well look at it. A lone hander is hardly likely to break in here, go through that business with the phone and fuses then pop out again to make the call and take a chance on getting back here at the right time. He...' He checked and frowned at Sander. 'What the hell's to grin at?'

Sander wiped off his weary grin and said: 'Notice anything just outside the place when you came in Dave?'

'What are you talking about?'

'There's a phone booth, bang outside. You can even see into that outer office when you're making a call.' The weary grin started to creep back. 'All part of the pattern of everything in this damned job.'

'And it would give this joker time to get in and out that quick?'

Sander nodded and then jerked his head at Blackman who was lounging just out of earshot. Blackman moved closer.

'What did that test come out at Gary from box back through window?'

'Less than half a minute gov. I did it twice. Same each time.'

'We're bloody jinxed,' Tripp muttered impatiently.

There was a moment's silence then Sander said with over-elaborate casualness.

'Where's the D.C.S.? I should have thought that he would have been in full flight round here by now.'

'Conference in the Midlands,' Tripp grunted. 'He does a lot of them. Not due back until after the weekend. Though this might bring him haring home.' He paused and a troubled look crept into his eyes. 'He'll want a scalp for this one Jack.'

'So I should imagine.' Sander was strangely uncaring.

There was another silence while Tripp fought an internal battle, then he said quietly. 'Though perhaps *we* can work something out before he arrives.'

Sander peered into his face then felt a quick surge of gratitude. So the old war-horse could not stay on the sidelines after all. Then he shook his head. It had been his plan. No one had twisted his arm. 'I doubt it. Anyway, I'll let you have a full report of the measures *I* took for security and surveillance before he gets back.'

The silence came back, then Tripp nodded and let out his breath heavily. 'Yes. Do that. And now I suppose I had better get hold of our lord and master. He won't be happy about this but he'll be a damned sight less happy if he hears it on the news or reads it in his paper.' He paused for a moment, then added: 'Sorry Jack,' before moving away.

Sander watched him go then turned to face Blackman's quizzical, intelligent face. 'Is this one down to us governor?' he asked shrewdly.

'Not, us, Gary – me.'

'But surely...'

'Let it drop Gary,' Sander said shortly, then relented at the concern on the other's face. 'Anyway, we've got a breathing space until after the weekend and with our brilliant deductions we might wrap it all up by then.'

'Yeah, and all the villains in the manor might come in, confess and give themselves up.' Blackman's tone matched his troubled face.

'We've still got the old man's story to come,' Sander reminded him. 'Could get lucky.'

The concern on Blackman's face changed to one of hesitant doubt. Self doubt.

Sander watched it for a moment then said: 'What is it?'

Blackman was still hesitant. 'This old man Munson, governor. I had an idea about him when I was climbing in and out of the window on that phone caper. He – well he could be tied into it.'

'How do you work that out?'

'Well, I thought, why an outside call at all? He could have just walked along and said there was a call.'

'And why would he do that?'

'The usual reason.' Blackman got a little more confident. 'I shouldn't think this job pays a fortune, and there's no golden handshake at the end of it. Let's face it, he's got the look of an old lag about him and once a lag, always a lag.'

Sander thought of at least two cutting remarks to shred the theory to bits, then checked. Had his own ideas been all that brilliant up to now? 'The prison reformers would love you. All right, I can see there's a bit more bubbling to come out – let's have it.'

'Well.' Blackman frowned while he marshalled his thoughts. 'Moving on from that, I got to thinking about how they knew about the set up – how they seemed to have known about everything from the start. With that old boy creeping around here with his ear to the ground, they could have found out a lot.'

Sander recalled the occasions when Munson had covered for Owen. He had certainly done enough to get his confidence. 'Hmm.

Yes, I suppose it fits – except that Munson's lying in hospital.'

Blackman's frown got a little deeper. 'Yeah – but then he wouldn't be the first one who got himself duffed up or slashed to make things look good afterwards,' he argued.

'Slashed?' Sander smiled. 'Do you see that blood out there?'

'It doesn't really prove anything gov.' Blackman was in full flight. 'I cut my hand slicing the joint one Sunday, I only had to have four stitches in it but that kitchen looked like a knacker's yard by the time I shot off to hospital.'

The statement made for more thought. 'But Caller said that he had passed out like a light,' Sander said slowly as though arguing with himself.

'Caller was concussed gov – and anyone can throw a dummy.'

Sander was silently thoughtful. The idea certainly held a lot of water. Or was it because he was in a position where he had to grasp at straws?

Blackman saw the doubt on his face and plunged on. 'And another thing's just hit me gov. This Munson was always available. You remember how he told us that he didn't come on until one? Well that means that he would have been off when Tooty bought it, around here when Big Charlie copped, free again the morning Den Hawkins was strangled and here again this afternoon when this lot blew up.' He finished with a burst and looked at Sander triumphantly.

The look suddenly checked Sander's own racing thoughts. Gary was over-reaching. Sander had been a detective long enough to know that almost any half-dozen, unconnected facts could be fitted into a theory which was already firm in the mind – easily, and usually wrongly. He put up a restraining hand. 'Whoa. Ease up. You'll have him doing all the jobs himself in a minute.'

Blackman too, knew that his conjectures were taking wild flight but he was too far committed and carried on recklessly. 'Well – all right then – why not? We only put one man at a time at each of these jobs. Perhaps there is only one man – Munson.'

Sander smiled a little grimly. 'One, slightly-built, little, old man with a limp pushing what – sixty?' he said cuttingly.

Blackman flushed, was silent for a moment, then continued doggedly. 'Ok gov. One little, old man. Why not? Take this job. He fakes the call, he's already fixed the lights and the phone, he clouts Caller and then walks up behind Owen because Owen's not expecting anything from him. After that, he cuts himself, throws the gloves and the knife up the hall and lays down and waits for Caller to trip over him.' Blackman checked and blinked as though suddenly surprised at where his heat-inspired, wildly-racing thoughts had taken him then finished a little weakly: 'It could be done gov, er, don't you think?'

The smile which had stayed on Sander's face slowly faded. It was still wild, just an explanation built up from a given situation, but Gary was right. It could be done. 'Let's get along to that hospital,' he said firmly.

In spite of his reservations, a touch of the excitement of the hunter on a warm trail had built up in Sander on the way to the hospital. Now it took a severe check as he looked down on the pallid, pain-lined face in the bed and took in the white sling and the drip-transfusion tube which led from it up to the bottle suspended by the bed.

'Hello Mr Sander,' Munson said in a voice that lacked a lot.

'How's it going then.' Sander's own voice had that false heartiness which always creeps in when a healthy person addresses the sick.

'Can't complain you know.'

'Feel up to talking?'

'Oh yes. I was going to tell your man who was sitting here when I came round but he said hang on until someone like you got here.'

'Well we timed it right then, didn't we. Ok, go ahead. Take your own time.' He nodded to Blackman who took out his notebook.

Munson waited politely until he was ready and then began in a weak, but firm, voice. 'Let's see. I suppose it started when I got that phone call asking for Mr Caller and the man on the other end saying that it was you that was calling when I tried to get through to Mr Owen's office and couldn't.'

'Did he sound like me?'

Munson frowned. 'Well it's hard to say now. I've never heard your voice all that much, Mr Sander, and people sound different on the phone. Then I was a bit surprised that you knew Mr Caller so I really didn't think about the voice. No – that's wrong isn't it? Not you. What I mean is, that he knew...'

'Yes, I understand,' Sander said. 'Then what?'

'I went along to tell Mr Caller.'

'Along the already-darkened passage?'

'Eh? Oh yeah. I'd had trouble with that already. I went along it just before the call to get a new booking-pad. We've got a bit of a storeroom just along there. The light was out then so I got a new bulb from the storeroom and tried that but it didn't make no difference. I'm no electrician but...'

'You were going for Mr Caller,' Sander reminded.

'Mm? Oh sorry. Well I told Mr Caller. He seemed surprised, but not all that. He told Mr Owen to leave the door open and followed me down the hall. He started to have a moan about the dark so I thought I'd have a look at the fuse box. Like I was saying, I'm not an electrician but I can mend a fuse. Anyway, when I got to the thing, I found it open and a bit of it was gone.'

'How did you see it?' Sander asked quietly.

'See it? Oh, in the dark you mean. Matches.'

Sander thought of the few spent matches some eagle-eye had noted near the fuse box and nodded. 'Then?'

'I stood by it for perhaps a minute or so wondering what was going on, maybe even longer, then I thought I'd better let Mr Owen know and went back into the main passage. The door at my office end was shut

195

but Mr Owen's was open. Then I saw this bloke coming out of it.'

Sander tensed slightly. 'What was he like?'

Munson shook his head. 'I can't really say. He had the office light behind him. You know the sort of thing. And I really didn't get time to look properly. He came down that passage like a rocket at me and we started a little set to.'

Sander looked at the slight form which looked even smaller in the wide bed. 'Took a bit of nerve.'

Munson grinned weakly. 'Not really Mr Sander. I'm no hero. He come so fast I couldn't get out the way – and there was nowhere to run to anyway. Well, anyway, I shouted for Mr Caller and sort of shoved at him and then he pushed me off and lifted his arm up. I couldn't really see anything in it but I put my own up to protect myself. Then I felt this real pain in my arm and felt that I was bleeding. It made me feel sick and light-headed. I tried to turn and run a bit and that's about the last I remember until I woke up here.'

Sander was silent for a moment, swallowing disappointment, then he said: 'And you didn't get a look at this man at all?'

'Not really. His face was just a sort of a

dark blur, you know. Sorry.'

'Was he short, tall, fat, thin?'

'Oh big. Blooming big. And strong too. He shoved me off like I was nothing.'

'Did he say anything?'

'Not a dicky-bird. One thing though. I think he was dark – dark-haired that is. When we struggled, the light from the office caught his hair and it looked dark. Oh, and he had sort of gloves on. Well something like gloves. They was very rough when he got hold of me.'

'Any ideas about anything else he was wearing?'

'Well his coat was rough. Like a tweed jacket feeling.'

Sander felt a little surprise. He did not really associate a tweed jacket with a character like this. 'Sure about that? Not leather or denim?'

'No. I'm pretty certain it was a sort of sports coat.'

Sander tucked the odd fact away in his mind with the others. A big man, dark-haired, sports coat. Then he got a wry grin behind his face as he realised he had automatically stopped thinking of Munson as a suspect. He took a quick look at Blackman and saw the same thing in his face.

'Oh well,' he said with forced heartiness. 'I think that will do for now Mr Munson. We'll want a written statement, of course, but that can come later when you've had a few days in here to pull yourself together.'

Munson shook his head vigorously. 'I'm not stopping here Mr Sander. I've got a bit of a thing about being boxed in and anyway...' He paused and looked at Sander directly. 'Mr Owen – he is...'

'Dead,' Sander supplied. 'Yes.'

'Poor bugger,' Munson said quietly. 'I thought he had to be but your man wouldn't say. Said not to bother about it until later.' He was silent for a moment, then shook his head again. 'Anyway, that settles it. I can't stop here. That means I'm out of graft now and I'll need to get signed on the sick and all that.'

Sander looked at the worried face and sighed lightly. So this had been his mass killer, worried about his Social Security? 'Just forget about that until you're better Mr Munson,' he advised and turned and tramped to the door.

Outside the door, he paused and looked at Sergeant Blackman. 'Well?'

Blackman looked back through the

observation panel in the door for a moment at the still figure on the other side. When he looked back to Sander, his face held a weak grin. 'I feel like a twat governor.'

Sander answered the grin. 'Well if it makes you feel any better Gary – so do I. But we started it so we might as well see it through to the bitter end.'

Doctor Vickers was a short, balding, irascible man who seemed to have little time for anything – least of all for police inspectors asking rather foolish questions.

'Self-inflicted?' he repeated with a curl of the lip which revealed what he thought of the question. 'Yes, technically possible, I suppose.' The lip curled a little more. 'That is if you consider your Mr Munson has enough cold-blooded nerve to drive a knife completely through his upper forearm so that it emerged on the inner side, bouncing off the bone and severing a variety of blood vessels on the way. Yes, quite technically possible – hmp.'

'Thank you doctor.' Sander kept his voice even and patient. He had encountered the very-busy-man syndrome before. 'Now, was Munson in any real danger from the wound?'

Doctor Vickers leaned back in his chair

and gazed hard at Sander to make sure that he really was dealing with a cretin. 'Only if you consider bleeding to death a *real* danger, Inspector.'

'And how near was he to that?'

Vickers considered for a moment. 'Hmm. Difficult to say exactly without knowing the position in which he was lying. Points of pressure and all that you know. But without the application of that rough tourniquet, five-perhaps ten minutes.' He fiddled impatiently with the papers in front of him. 'Now, if there's nothing else Inspector?'

'Not from me, thank you doctor,' Sander looked at Blackman. 'Gary?'

'Nor from me,' Blackman assured him fervently.

14

Sander perched on the edge of a desk in the incident room, swung an idle leg and watched a pretty, dark, W.P.C. divide her attention between the sheaf of paperwork in her hand and the new blackboard in front of her.

Another blackboard; another set of figures, facts, photographs, sketches and plans; another laboriously traced road to nowhere.

Not only the blackboard was new this morning, there was also a new atmosphere in the incident room. It was a compound of weariness – here we go down that same old trail again – and a faint, gossipy excitement. The grapevine was already buzzing with the unconfirmed rumour that the head of Inspector Jack Sander was on the chopping block because of this last fiasco. Sander had seen it in the faces as he walked through the room. The deliberately non-committal, the faintly sympathetic and, just here and there, a touch of smug satisfaction. Now, he could feel it washing against his broad back. Oh well, they would all know for sure after the weekend and the return of Unwin, hot on the trail of someone to burn to make a suitable smoke screen.

'Nice, eh governor?' a cheerful voice said over his shoulder and turned slightly to look into the deliberately bright face of Sergeant Blackman watching the trim back of the W.P.C.

'I thought you went in for blondes,' he replied, matching the tone.

'Oh I like to give them all a fair crack of the whip,' Blackman, said loftily.

Sander smiled, grateful for the lightness and the implicit support. A good man, Gary. As Sander's chosen assistant, some of the mud from this affair was bound to rub off on him – and he knew it.

'Anything new from forensic?' he asked, remembering the order of tasks he had allotted Blackman on the previous evening.

Blackman sniffed, got a slightly disgusted expression and pulled out his notebook. 'They say,' he said, peering at the book and matching his voice to his expression, 'that death occurred during diastolic action of the heart or at the moment between diastole and systole, which apparently means that he died instantly which we could have told them anyway. Just bloody showing off, I think.'

'Nothing else?'

'Nothing we didn't know. Double-edged weapon, delivery of death stroke and absence of preliminary attempts would indicate that killer was steady-nerved and practised in the art, and so on and so on.' He closed the note-book with a snap. 'A fancy way of saying that this joker knew what he was about.'

'And that we knew as well,' Sander grunted and eyed the blackboard before moving on to the others. 'So now we've got an expert gunman, an expert strangler, an expert bomber, and an expert shiv man. A very useful collection of talented gentlemen.'

'Or a top-trained secret-agent who has retired and now only does part-time work,' Blackman offered with a grin.

'Or a KGB defector who is short of a bob or two,' Sander contributed.

'Or an S.A.S. man who has gone into business on his own,' Blackman capped.

'Or Uncle Tom Cobbleigh and all,' Sander finished, sighed, then let his eyes wander to the plastic flower in Blackman's button-hole. 'You going to a wedding, or something?'

'Leave it out governor. It's a poppy. Remembrance Sunday. Day after tomorrow.'

'Oh yes. So it is. Bit previous, aren't you?'

Blackman's grin got a little wider. 'Well there's this civvy secretary up in the collating office who sells them and sort of pressed me into having one this morning. I couldn't turn down a good cause like that.'

'Of course not,' Sander said heavily. 'Particularly with her snuggling up against you while she fitted it into your lapel. Let's see, she's dark as well isn't she? Big, soft, brown eyes.'

'Now you come to mention it, I think she is governor,' Blackman remembered with massive innocence.

'There'll be a sheet out here on you one day,' Sander told him. 'Indecent exposure, I should think.'

'You can't make that stick between consenting adults governor.'

Sander matched the grin on Blackman's face. 'All right, I give up. Now we had better get on with some work. You can see if there is any house to house stuff in yet and start going through that.'

'Ok. Do you want anything likely passed straight over to you.'

'Not for a while,' Sander said grimly. 'I've got a long report to write.'

It was a long report and it got more difficult

as it grew under his two-fingered typing. Stated baldly, he did not have much of a defence and there were many aspects to cover – even to working out some sort of alibi for Blackman. Some white lie to the effect that he had protested Sander's procedures.

His eyes wandered to Blackman, his head bent over a nearby desk, and again picked up the scarlet poppy in his lapel. Was it really that late in the year? And where had it gone? He grimaced slightly – on master Owen mainly. It must have been about this time last year when he had really begun to concentrate on him – the time of that affair of the bank raid and the death of that young man. The death of that young man...

A tiny bubble of an idea popped into his mind.

He ignored it but it swelled again, even stronger, and he took his eyes from Blackman and switched them to the line of blackboards and let the thought range and grow until it began to pick up with others. It was almost ridiculous – but...

'Gary,' he called quietly.

Blackman looked up, noted the expression on his face, then got up and crossed to him, resting his knuckles on the desk. 'Yes governor?'

Sander picked his words slowly to match his ranging thoughts. 'That bank job last year when the kid got blasted. The one we put down to Owen. When was it – November – December?'

Blackman prided himself on his memory and his reply was instant. 'December. Couple of weeks before Christmas and as cold as bloody charity. Name of, er, Maxwell.'

'That's right,' Sander said and was silent so long that Blackman stirred uneasily.

'Anything else gov?'

'Eh?' Sander lifted his head to look at him. 'Oh, yes. There was a brother-in-law, or something, we ran into, remember?'

'That's right. The woman's brother, the boy's uncle. Big, dark, stroppy bloke. Sergeant-major type. All for bringing back the cat and hanging and shooting every...' Blackman paused then said quietly: 'Oh no.'

'Oh no, what?' Sander's voice was just as quiet.

'Oh no, not me yesterday and you today gov.'

The comment checked Sander's wide-ranging thoughts. Gary was right. He too was painting pictures in the sky framed in facts tailored to fit. Odd how it was always so readily apparent to the bystander. But he could not let the idea go.

'All right Gary. So I'm just as guilty. But let's have a think about it. How would you very quickly sum up this whole case up till now?'

'Kinky,' Blackman said shortly.

'Yeah. I was thinking of weird, but it amounts to the same thing. Weird the way the crimes are committed; weird the way we get no word from the underworld crew; weird the timing; and, weirdest of all, the apparent lack of motive. All right, let's think weird. We get a weird answer – but it's an answer to everything. Motive, manner, timing, everything.'

Sander watched the thoughts chase across Blackman's face and watched him get impressed in spite of himself.

'So you are supposing that someone – say this sergeant-major...'

'A big, dark man,' Sander reminded him quietly. 'With half a lifetime of weapon training behind him.'

'My S.A.S. man eh?'

'That helped give the idea birth but he would be a commando or a paratrooper in his day.'

'True. So this trained killer, who happens to fit the one sketchy description we've got, starts a one man war against Owen and his mob in revenge for what they did to his nephew. Is that it?'

'A nephew who, I seem to remember, he thought of as a son,' Sander put in.

Blackman visibly cast his mind back. 'Ye-es. There was something to that effect, wasn't there. And the whole thing timed to finish up on the anniversary of the original killing?'

'That was the real germ of the idea. It was mixed and muddled in my mind but I've had this thing all along about the timing of these killings. I still think that Owen was intended to be the grand finale in December but this boy was adaptable enough to change course when he saw what we were up to and took advantage of it. He's still got Fred Dew to keep to schedule with.'

'Kinky,' Blackman said without thinking.

'You said it, not me,' Sander reminded him.

'Yes, I did, didn't I,' Blackman said thoughtfully. 'I don't know though.' He paused and looked doubtfully at Sander.

'Spit it out,' Sander advised him.

'Well it all fits – but this lad would be a bit long in the tooth for this sort of caper, wouldn't he gov?' In Blackman's voice was the conviction that the young, fit and strong have, that anyone, even slightly older, is getting near to decrepit.

Sander half-smiled at the sentiment behind the words. It was unintentional, but it fitted him as well. Then he shook his head firmly. 'Think of your poppy and Remembrance Day, Gary.'

'What the hell have they got to do with it?'

'They were part of a sort of subconscious knowledge that helped the idea on. I pictured all those old lads you see in the march past. Drab-suited, bowler-hatted, and getting a little past it, but most of them with a line of medals showing that they have probably killed more men than all our home-grown villains put together.'

'That's a thought,' Blackman agreed, digesting a new concept.

'And it put our man in an era when wartime souvenirs were two a penny.'

'Bombs, guns, knives. Yes, that's another thought.'

'I'll give you a final one.' Sander grinned. 'This lad would be about the same age, size and weight as the D.C.I. How does that grab you?'

Blackman pictured the craggy, Chief Inspector Tripp, then nodded shortly. 'He's capable.'

'Which leaves us with just one snag.'

'What's that gov?'

'For the life of me, I can't think of the man's name. You?'

Blackman furrowed his brow and shook his head. 'No. Damned if I can. And it won't be worth looking in the files, there was never any reason for him to go down.'

'But he did have a sister,' Sander thought aloud.

'I'll get the car,' Blackman said eagerly and looked at him for confirmation.

Sander was quiet for a moment. On reflection, there were a lot of holes. Too many damned holes. Then his thoughts moved on what else he had to go on and the likelihood of anything else emerging before the close of the weekend. 'Yes. You do that Gary.'

'I think we've had it gov,' Sergeant Blackman said after the fifth abortive push on the door-bell button.

Sander nodded and looked thoughtfully at the new, modern curtains at the windows and the child's scooter tucked under the front bay-window ledge. 'In more ways than one perhaps. But there was a neighbour, wasn't there?'

Blackman scrubbed his chin. 'That's right.

A Mrs – Mrs – Chel something. Chelsfield. Yeah, that was it. What do you fancy, right or left?'

Sander looked at the house on the right with its dirty step and windows and thought of the neat, bustling woman. 'Left.'

The woman looked at him with a puzzled air for a moment. 'Yes?' Then the air cleared and recognition dawned. 'Why, it's the Inspector, isn't it. Inspector – mm...'

'Sander,' he supplied. 'Good afternoon Mrs Chelsfield, we are...'

'Checksfield,' she corrected. 'Mrs Checksfield.'

'Oh yes. Silly of me. Sorry. As I was saying Mrs Checksfield.' Sander paused long enough to give Blackman a hard look and for Blackman to fix his eyes on an imaginary object some six inches above the top of his head. 'We are trying to locate Mrs Maxwell. We...' He paused again and looked at Mrs Checksfield's expression. 'Something wrong Mrs Checksfield?'

The woman shook her head at him and clicked her tongue. 'Of course there is – oh, but then you wouldn't know, would you? – there's no way that you could.'

'Know what?' Sander asked a little weakly.

'Why, about Mrs Maxwell. She's passed over, poor soul.'

'Dead you mean? When was this?'

'Well let me see now. Oh I'm terrible with dates. Our Lorna had... No, it was before that. Anyway, just after the New Year – couldn't have been long after. Flu, followed by chest infection of some sort, they said it was. But I knew better than that. Big, strong woman like that going with flu. Oh no. She'd lost the will to live – that was the real trouble. I said to my Bob, that poor soul has lost the will to live now that her last son has gone.'

Sander looked at the woman with a grave face. Under all that chatter, she was probably right. 'I see. I'm sorry to hear all that. What about Mr Maxwell?'

'He's gone too.'

'Dead?'

'Eh?' Mrs Checksfield looked puzzled for a moment and then her face cleared. 'Oh – Lord bless you, no. Gone from here. Mr Chapman took him with him.'

The name suddenly registered. 'His brother-in-law?'

'That's right. Fancy you remembering. Yes, Harry Chapman.' Mrs Checksfield paused and nodded her head approvingly.

'And it was a kind thing to do. But then I don't suppose that he could have done much else really, the state the poor man was in.'

'In a bad way was he?'

'Oh shocking. You'd never believe. He was bad enough after they lost their boy but when she went, he just went to pieces completely. Sort of, in on himself, if you know what I mean. As though no one else was there like.'

Sander nodded. 'Do you know where they went?'

She shook her head vigorously. 'Never did Inspector. I wanted to ask but Mr Chapman wasn't the sort of man you chatted to a lot. Sort of brusque. Still, he must have had a kind heart underneath it all. I said to my Bob at the time, you never know about people from the outside. You look...'

Mrs Checksfield's voice droned on.

Blackman ducked into the far side of the squad car but Sander paused at the kerb and looked back at the little house. It had certainly known its share of grief. Grief which might have given Chapman an added incentive. Now he had a sister to avenge as well. He shook his head slowly. 'Vengeance is mine,' said the Lord, and the law of the land agreed but – perhaps this family was owed a vengeance?

The policeman in him warred with the human being for a moment, then he shook his head again and slid into the car to meet the receiver which Blackman held out to him.

'Message for you gov. Urgent it seems.'

Sander took the instrument and grunted: 'Sander – over.'

'Will Inspector Sander please contact the businessman as soon as possible. Message understood? Over,' the tinny, mechanical voice rattled.

Sander was thoughtfully silent for a moment, then said: 'Understood – over and out,' and replaced the receiver and frowned at it.

Blackman watched his face for a moment then made an educated guess. 'You got a new snout governor?'

'It looks very much like it Gary,' Sander said slowly.

'Want me to make a start on hunting up this Chapman character while you are with him?'

Sander was very thoughtful again, then shook his head. 'No. I think it might be as well to have you along on this one.' He nodded confirmation to himself. 'Yes. Ok Gary, let's go and see the businessman.'

15

Sander laid the sheet of paper Bowyer had given him carefully on the desk between them. 'Mm. Very nice writing – but apart from that, it doesn't mean a lot.'

Bowyer looked at the paper and began, as though reading it upside down. 'The first one's a car number, Mr Sander. Dark-blue Granada. It's owned by Joe Waylett's old woman – or the slag who used to be Joe's old woman.'

Sander noted the choice of words silently. 'That's nice for her. Go on.'

'The next is a little body shop in Cardross Road. Micky Pope's place. Does a nice job, does Micky, but a bit bent and a bit greedy.' Bowyer's voice was flat and even.

'That a fact? I must remember not to take my next wallop down there. So?'

'So the day after Joe got whacked down someone brought a car into Micky with a dented wing, smashed headlight and a bent bumper. Said they wanted a quick job on it. Even gave Micky a few quid to go straight

216

on through the night on it if he had to.'

'That's interesting.'

'It gets more interesting Mr Sander. Like I said, this Micky's a bit greedy. He could have banged the wing out but the man said, quick, and a new wing was the quickest, so Micky fitted one and shoved this barely damaged wing up the back of his shop to beat out and make a few bob out of later. It's still there and still got signs of whatever dented it on it.'

Sander felt himself stiffening behind his impassive face. 'You were right. It does get more interesting. Who was this careless driver with a lot of money to throw about?'

Bowyer's face was equally impassive. 'Vince Amato.'

'Well – well,' Sander said quietly and looked at the paper again. 'And this last?'

'That's the address of a quiet, little flat where Vince and this slag are shacked up. They've been going there on and off for some time apparently.' Bowyer paused for a moment, then added. 'They're probably there this evening.'

'Convenient.' Sander lifted his eyes to look directly at Bowyer. 'And I take it that you had an idea of this when you promoted this nut case up here where you could keep an eye on him?'

Bowyer permitted himself a slight smile. 'An inkling, Mr Sander, an inkling.'

'And that Amato is still too well connected for you to chance a split in the organisation by taking him out on your own?' Sander queried spitefully.

Bowyer's smile died. 'No sense in making unnecessary waves Mr Sander.'

'Poor business, eh?'

'Something like that.' Bowyer shrugged. 'Or perhaps I'm just doing my duty as a citizen and a tax payer?'

'Yes, and I'm coming up for the Nobel Peace Prize next year,' Sander sniffed, then straightened and reached for the paper. 'But in the meantime, we can use this. All right Bowyer, we'll take Amato off your back for you.'

He folded the paper and slipped it into his pocket, experiencing a slight feeling of let down. True, this was very useful and it cleared up one factor in the case. Might even make Mr Unwin look at him with less threat in his eyes on Monday – might. But he had somehow expected more. His gaze crossed Bowyer's as he pulled his coat together. Then perhaps there was more?

'That the lot?' he asked casually.

Bowyer pulled at the end of his chin. 'There's a bit of suss – a few whispers – but I don't know whether you'd be interested in that Mr Sander.'

'Try me. I'm a very sympathetic listener.'

'Well it seems that Vince was quite put out when I let Owen get away with a bit. You know how touchy these young tearaways are. Seems he made a few threats about going after them on his own at the time. Some people think that he might have seen the chance to start a bit of a war, grab Joe's missus and Joe's job in the confusion and, perhaps, even move up a bit higher than that. Fishing in troubled waters, I think they call it.'

'I think they do,' Sander said guardedly. 'But like you say, just suss and whispers – or is it?'

'Couple of funny things to back it. Seems Vince has got a bit of a liking for trips to the Smoke – started making them round about the beginning of August and it also looks like he might have made certain that he was with a lot of people at certain times.'

'What certain times?' Sander's voice was low.

'Times when things were happening.'

'For instance?'

'Oh, like taking a party to Ascot the day of that factory raid, or starting a bit of bother in a crowded billiard hall on the morning Hawkins was topped, or making a bit of a scene in an afternoon disco a few days ago – the day Owen got shivved.'

'You left out the night Big Charlie went up with a bang,' Sander pointed out.

Bowyer's lips tightened. 'The saucy bastard wangled himself an invite to my house,' he gritted.

A grim grin pulled at Sander's lips, then died as his thoughts raced on. This certainly gave a new look to everything. All right, it knocked out his theory about Harry Chapman but he would have no regrets about that. He looked hard at Bowyer. 'Is this all straight info?'

'It ought to be,' Bowyer grunted. 'It bloody well cost enough.'

'Anything else?'

'No. That's it.'

Sander carried on looking hard. Just enough to wet the appetite eh? But it was too much to be ignored. 'All right, we'll look into it,' he grunted as he got to his feet, then added as a grudging afterthought. 'Thanks.'

'Anytime Mr Sander,' Bowyer said pleasantly then his voice lifted as Sander began to turn away. 'I take it that's fulfilled our deal?'

Sander checked and looked down at him. 'I don't remember any deal.'

Bowyer smiled. 'Of course not. But, er these lads of yours have been cramping people's style a bit over the last few weeks. I thought you might see your way clear to calling them off now.'

The memory of the little house he had visited popped into Sander's mind as he continued to gaze down at the smooth, smiling face. What had happened there was directly attributable to men like this one. There were brutal crooks, smiling crooks, clever crooks – but there were no good crooks. 'Bowyer,' he said evenly, 'if we have made life awkward for you over the past weeks, then I'm bloody glad. And if I can get them to go on doing it that way, then I bloody will.'

He waited long enough to enjoy the quick anger that flooded into Bowyer's face then turned and tramped out.

Bowyer looked at the door that had closed behind Sander long enough to master his temper, then he took a large cigar, lit it, leaned back and puffed slowly and contemplatively. Thirty minutes dragged by on leaden feet this way but none registered on Bowyer's impassive face. Then the telephone rang.

'Bowyer,' he said into the receiver.

'They're here boss,' a hoarse voice answered in his ear.

He paused for a moment as though making a final decision, then said firmly. 'All right. Give him a bell and tell him what I told you to say.'

In a telephone box close to a low, select block of flats, a man watched Sander and Blackman push through the swing doors then he carefully dialled a number, listened to it ring, then began to talk. He had a hoarse voice.

The bell was ringing as Sander and Blackman walked the short hall and stopped a few moments before they arrived at the door they were looking for.

Blackman pressed the door buzzer three times at intervals and got nothing but blank silence in return then he looked at Sander. 'That phone bell stopped in mid-ring gov,' he said quietly. 'Sounded as though it might have been from in here.'

Sander nodded agreement. 'All right

Gary, let's make out we're on the telly. Clog it.'

Blackman grinned, stepped back, raised his arms for balance then lifted a brawny leg and slammed it against the door lock.

The lock tore from splintering wood, but half-held until Sander's beefy shoulder completed the task and he plunged forward into the room. Experience sent him in hard and low and instinct sent him to the right away from the partially-open door. Too many people had been clobbered by others standing behind doors. The automatic action saved his life.

There was an explosive crack that seemed to rupture his eardrums followed immediately by a second; a woman half-screamed; and Blackman gave a short cry then swore viciously.

All of this he heard as he launched himself towards the cover of a low settee close to the door. He hit the carpet in a knee-jarring scramble then reached out to steady a tottering standard-lamp which had partially impeded his progress finding time to almost laugh in a tiny corner of his mind at the normalcy of the reaction. Other sensations chased through his mind. The thought that he was getting too old for a damned caper like this followed quickly by self-anger at the quick fear the shots had built in him followed again by sudden concern as he mentally arranged the sequence of events.

He twisted in the direction of the open door. 'Gary – you all right?'

'Nicked a bit governor – but I'll live.' Blackman's voice was tightly held over a faint tremble. 'What goes on?'

'That's what I'd like to know,' Sander grunted as the concern changed back to anger, then he lifted his voice to bawl across the room. 'Amato – what the bloody hell do you think you're playing at?'

There was a fractional pause then Amato called back; 'Sander?' His voice tailing up into slight disbelief.

'Who did you think it was – Father bloody Christmas?' Sander growled.

There was another pause, then Amato barked a short, hard laugh and said. 'Conned – bleeding conned – and like a mug I bought it.'

Sander frowned at the words. 'What?'

The laugh repeated. 'Let it ride copper – my business.'

'And this is mine,' Sander growled then forced his voice down to normal. 'Now look Amato. This is stupid. Half this block of flats will have rung in about those shots by now and in a few minutes there'll be more cars jammed round here than you can shake a stick at. Give it up. You're not going anywhere. Slide that gun across the floor and jack this nonsense in.'

'You'd love that wouldn't you Sander. The big hero. I can see it all now. But you're wrong as usual. I am going somewhere. I'm going out of that door – now – before this crowd of yours arrive. I'm going slow and easy Sander and you and your oppo outside had better remember that they can't do much more to me now if I finish the pair of you off, so play it smart and keep well out of the way.' His voice lifted. 'You outside – did you get an earful of that?'

'Vince – what about me?' a quavering, woman's voice asked.

'Sod you darling,' Amato rapped. 'All right Sander, I'm coming. Keep your nut down if you know what's good for you buster.'

Sander bent lower, strained his hearing, and heard Amato's feet start to slide across the carpet. It was not a sound that gave him confidence. Not slow enough to show fear and not fast enough to denote panic. His own fear, which had never quite left him, began to build again. Amato was wrong. He was not a big hero. But then he couldn't let this head-case with a gun in his hand out onto the streets.

He cast round for something – anything – then saw his hand still gripping the standard-lamp.

The toe of a suede shoe slid into view then bent as it took the weight of the body above it. It should be about now – it had to be about now. Sander tipped the lamp into the path of the advancing shoe.

He heard Amato swear; saw another foot tangle in the length of the lamp; then saw him flounder to the floor. He scrambled forward but Amato was twisting like a cat, his gun flailing, his face a wedge of angry hate, and he had the sudden, certain knowledge that he was never going to make it in time. Then a big figure jumped through the doorway.

Gary Blackman's face was white and his right hand, stained red, clasped the upper part of his left arm. Neither stopped him dropping on both knees with a thud into Amato's back.

The breath pumped out of him explosively and his face went forward into the carpet.

Still half-upright, Sander scrambled on and hit him just behind the jaw as hard as he

226

had ever punched anyone in his life.

'You all right gov,' Blackman gasped from his kneeling position.

Sander looked into the concern on the face that was so close it seemed larger than life. 'I'll never be the bloody same again,' he wheezed in a voice which failed dismally to mask a definite tremble.

16

The police station was alive with early, Saturday evening activity. The football hooligans were coming in; the busy-Saturday-afternoon shoplifters were being interviewed; and the rest of the station was girding itself up for Saturday night. The drunks, the violence and the mindless vandalism.

Seated in his office, cheeks supported in cupped hands, Sander heard it without really taking it in. He was exhausted. It had been a long night, broken by only a few hours sleep, and an even longer day. Amato was not the kind of man who broke easily. It had taken hour upon hour of questioning; of going over the same ground; of slowly demolishing the lies and evasions. Sander sighed. And all for nothing.

He sighed again then straightened and pulled out a cigarette. The smoke from it brought a blink from the eyes which were already too full of smoke and seemingly lined at the back with grains of sand. He puffed again, then looked at it severely.

'Bloody things,' he muttered then lifted the tired eyes to where the door of the office was opening.

'Hello gov,' Blackman said. He wore a wide grin and a white sling.

Sander frowned. 'Hello. I thought you were still fighting for life in an intensive care unit?'

The grin stayed. 'No gov. I've had it there. Once those photographers started coming in, that was it. Those hospital nightshirts don't do a damned thing for my image.'

In spite of his tiredness, Sander smiled, then the smile shifted to concern. 'And you're all right?'

'Sure gov. Just a deep gouge across the fleshy part of the upper arm. I've done worse shaving.' The grin popped back again. 'Mind you, I might feel a bit of a relapse coming on round about Monday when the Chief Super gets back.'

'Lucky old you,' Sander said with feeling.

Blackman noted it and his face sobered. 'How did we do?'

'We didn't,' Sander grunted.

'You mean he didn't fake a hit and run?'

'Oh yeah, we got him on that all right. The bird coughed, the wing's down with forensic and he's included it in his final statement.

We've also got him on possession, wounding with intent, picking his nose out of season, and half-a-dozen other things – but for the rest – that was just Mr Bowyer being bloody clever and making sure that Amato went down for a lot longer than hit and run would have got him.' He puffed at the cigarette and leaned forward a little. 'That phone we heard. That was someone tipping Amato that Bowyer was on to him and a couple of imported heavies were on their way to see to him.'

'Clever bastard,' Blackman said without heat. 'Can we prove anything?'

'With just a rough voice over the phone and Bowyer protesting innocence and vowing to find out who the grass in his organisation is? – do me a favour.'

'Yeah, I see what you mean.' Blackman bit his lower lip thoughtfully. 'So we're back to square one.'

'What square – what one?'

'This Chapman geezer.'

'Oh sure.' The way Sander felt was in his voice. 'All we have to do is find out where he is and get a cough out of him – and all before Monday.'

'We can start to look for him gov,' Blackman urged, worried by the lack of life in the seated figure.

'Starting where?'

'Well – there's the army people for a start. If he was a long server he might be copping a pension. They'd have an address on him.'

'And they are going to turn out Saturday night or Sunday to dig it out for us? Be your age Gary.' Sander ground out the cigarette viciously then he looked at Blackman and his expression softened. 'No. I appreciate you coming back and wanting to help Gary – and I mean that. But let's face it son – we've had it. You shoot off and rest that arm which is quite all right but makes you wince when you move it.'

Blackman grinned weakly, looked down at the offending arm and then reached over to tuck, in the battered poppy, half dragged out by the sling. Then his hand checked. 'The Legion,' he said.

'That's where I'll probably finish up,' Sander agreed sourly.

'No gov. The British Legion. It's a quid to nothing that a military bod like this one will be a member. They'll have something on him at the local branch. An address – something like that.'

Sander looked at the excited face and felt new life begin to stir in his own jaded mind.

'You're a bugger for overtime, aren't you?' he said with a grin that had some of that new life in it. 'Come on – this time, I'll drive you.'

Sander and Blackman stood in the doorway of the hall and looked at the apparent sea of pressed suits, medal ribbons, and even medals, then Sander frowned at Blackman. 'Is it always like this on Saturday night?'

Blackman shrugged. 'Search me gov. I shouldn't think so though. Looks more like some gala night.'

Sander nodded and his eyes swept over the room again then checked as they hooked onto a familiar face. 'We can find out over there,' he said and started across the hall.

Police Sergeant Bowdery straightened and turned from the bar in answer to the tap on his shoulder. For a moment, he looked surprised then got a smile on his face. 'Hello Inspector, what are you doing here? Hello Gary. Up and about again are you?'

'Struggling on manfully.'

Bowdery's smile widened. 'You'll make Super yet son.' He turned back to Sander. 'Drink Inspector?'

'I'll have a half of bitter with you Phil.'

'And you?' Bowdery looked at Blackman. 'Pint as usual, I suppose – guts?'

'Never could manage halves Phil, you know that.'

Bowdery sniffed, ordered the drinks.

'Bit packed aren't you?' Sander offered after they had arrived and been tested.

'Big night Inspector, isn't it?' Bowdery looked at the puzzlement still on Sander's face. 'Remembrance Day eve.'

'Oh – yes – so it is.'

'Always an occasion here Inspector. Some branches don't but we like to make a big thing of it. Full turn out – even decorations – all that sort of thing.'

'Nice,' Sander murmured with faint interest, his eyes scanning the crowd.

Bowdery watched him with shrewd eyes then remembered his original question. 'You didn't say what you are doing here Inspector.'

Sander was silent for a moment, sorting his thoughts carefully. There was only the theory that he and Gary had cooked up and that looked more improbable by the minute in this festive atmosphere. It could be very dodgy ground.

'Mm? Oh, just sort of fishing, I suppose. It's these Owen killings. Someone suggested

233

that they've got the hallmark of a trained man. Commando, Special Services, that sort of thing. We thought that this would be the most likely place where we could have a quiet chat with some experienced men who might be able to confirm the idea. Looks like we picked the wrong night though. As a matter of fact, the same someone said that we might look up a Harry Chapman down here. Apparently he's a bit of an expert on these things and...' He broke off and stared at Bowdery's grinning face. 'Did I say something funny?'

'Too bloody right you did,' Bowdery chuckled, then composed his face. 'Sorry Inspector. I know Harry Chapman – most of us do – and the thought of him being an expert on violence...' His face started to go again and he repeated a half-choked, 'Sorry again,' as he tried to control it.

Sander kept his own face and voice deliberately light. 'Duff info, eh?'

Bowdery had another go at his face and nodded. 'As duff as you can get. Whoever told you to look up Harry, was out of his mind. Oh sure, Harry was in the kate for years and talks a good fight but he was never in anything else but supply. I doubt if he even picked up a weapon after he marched out of basic training except to do a cere-monial with. If you want to talk to some lads who know, I could introduce you around, but not Harry, Inspector – not Harry.'

'Perhaps another evening when there's no party on then,' Sander said casually and caught the disappointment mirrored in Blackman's eyes as he bent his own over his glass. That was it then.

'Glad to Inspector – glad to,' Bowdery said and half-turned from the bar to look round the hall. 'There's plenty to choose from. Tommy Case over there. Bert Smedley, now he's a...' He checked for a moment. 'Hello, talk of the devil, here comes your expert now.' He checked again and a pleased ex-pression crept over his face. 'And he's got my old mate with him. That's great. He hasn't been here for a long time but I knew he wouldn't miss tonight. Now that *is* the man you really ought to have a word with In-spector if you want to know what it is all about. Got more medals than a Chelsea Pensioner, a commando in North Africa, did special work dodging in and out of those Greek Islands, fought in Burma, got cap-tured by the Japs and, bugger me, even escaped from them when he was half dead by shamming that he really was even when the bastards stuck bayonets into his legs to see if he reacted. That's what you call an expert fighting man, Inspector. Oh, but I forgot, you probably know him anyway, don't you? – that bank business last year when he lost his last boy. That was rough, he...'

Bowdery's voice carried on but neither Sander or Blackman was listening any more. They were both staring across the hall at the small, slim figure, his chest smothered with medal ribbons, standing beside the bulky Chapman. He still had that slightly worried expression, still stood with that half stooped, deferential air, still carried his left arm in a hospital sling.

Blackman let the air whistle out of his parted lips and said softly: 'Well I'll be double damned – Inspector...'

'Sod this job,' Inspector Jack Sander said with real feeling.

The publishers hope that this book has given you enjoyable reading. Large Print Books are especially designed to be as easy to see and hold as possible. If you wish a complete list of our books please ask at your local library or write directly to:

Dales Large Print Books
Magna House, Long Preston,
Skipton, North Yorkshire.
BD23 4ND

This Large Print Book, for people
who cannot read normal print,
is published under the auspices of

THE ULVERSCROFT FOUNDATION

... we hope you have enjoyed this book.
Please think for a moment about those
who have worse eyesight than you ...
and are unable to even read or enjoy
Large Print without great difficulty.

You can help them by sending a
donation, large or small, to:

**The Ulverscroft Foundation,
1, The Green, Bradgate Road,
Anstey, Leicestershire, LE7 7FU,
England.**
or request a copy of our brochure for
more details.

The Foundation will use all donations
to assist those people who are visually
impaired and need special attention
with medical research, diagnosis
and treatment.

Thank you very much for your help.